The Anastasia Trials in the Court of Women

An Interactive Comedy in Two Acts

Carolyn Gage

A SAMUEL FRENCH ACTING EDITION

SAMUEL FRENCH

FOUNDED 1830

SAMUELFRENCH.COM
SAMUELFRENCH-LONDON.CO.UK

MUSIC USE NOTE

INTRODUCTION

Women's roles have undergone dramatic changes in the West since the 1950's, and with these changes have come changes in our expectations of ourselves and each other. What are the limits of "sisterhood" as women move away from our status as fellow victims, toward more personal economic independence and autonomy?

This was a question for me when I wrote *The Anastasia Trials in the Court of Women*. I wanted to explore the radical changes in the interpersonal ethics practiced by women at the turn of the new century, and I especially wanted to explore the issue of betrayal.

In this play, five women are put on trial for their failure to recognize Anastasia Romanov after she escaped the massacre at Ekaterinburg and surfaced in a public mental asylum in Germany four years later. The women included a nurse at the asylum, her former nanny, an indigent fellow inmate, a former member of the royal court, and an American millionairess who hosted the Grand Duchess in New York. All of these women recognized Anastasia initially and then, responding to her history of trauma, rejected her later.

All of the women had reasons for their betrayals. They were all threatened with very real losses: loss of a job, loss of a husband, even loss of a life. On the other hand, the woman they betrayed was a deeply disturbed survivor — incapable of advocating for herself, suicidal, and desperate for recognition. On still another hand, Anastasia's post-traumatic behaviors were hostile and antisocial to such a degree that she compromised every effort made on her behalf by her supporters.

The Anastasia Trials is a play written at a pivotal point in the history of women. It has one foot in the patriarchal world where women accept the necessity of betraying each other, and one foot in the brave new world of testing the limits of our empowerment by standing in solidarity with each other, and especially with the survivors. It also stands at the turning point after the Second Wave, where it has become apparent that the rhetoric of sisterhood is not enough to reconcile the divisions between women caused by class and race. Were the utopian experiments of the radical feminists a failure because of that? Were all our achievements superficial? Where do we go from here?

The Anastasia Trials answers its own question in its challenge to traditional assumptions about a male-identified audience. The play is audience-interactive, but only with the women in the house. The men are not invited to vote on either the motions or the final verdict. The actors in the play continually address their arguments to "the women of the jury." In inviting the women of the audience to serve as judge and jury, *The Anastasia Trials* affirms a culture of, for, about, and serving the interests of women. It also acknowledges the presence of the audience, making explicit their contribution toward the creation of this culture and respecting their right to their own conclusions.

The radical format of *The Anastasia Trials* affirms a faith in the evolution of a women's culture that breaks down the hierarchical wall between the observer and the observed, the actor and the acted upon. It posits a culture where every woman's opinion carries weight, and where, even if perfect equality is an unrealizable goal, the progress toward it can be dynamic and self-interrogating.

This play is dedicated to Hyacinth Morgan,
a courageous survivor and a friend.

CAST OF CHARACTERS

BETTY: A butch stagehand, plays the Bailiff.

DIANE: The founder and director of the Emma Goldman Theater Brigade, plays the Prosecuting Attorney.

ATHENA: The daughter of a rich man, plays the Defense Attorney and also Annie Jennings, a wealthy socialite.

JENNY: An actor with stomach flu, plays Anastasia Romanov, and also the Prosecuting Attorney.

MELISSA: An actor bent on impressing the critics, plays Thea Malinowsky, a nurse from a public mental asylum.

MARIE: A grassroots, radical activist, plays Clara Peuthart, an alcoholic bag lady.

AMY: An actor with professional aspirations, plays Baroness Sophie Buxhoeveden, former lady-in-waiting to Anastasia's mother.

DONNA: An actor who resents Diane's authority, plays Shura Tegleva, Anastasia's former nursemaid.

LISA: The playwright, plays Baroness Zinaida Tolstoy, a former friend to Anastasia's mother and Anastasia.

SCENE
A stage set for a courtroom trial.

TIME
The present.

Each copy of the program for the play should contain a sheet of red paper and a sheet of green paper, along with a note that reads:
> "The women in the audience are invited to serve as judge and jury in the Court of Women."

ACT I

(The stage is bare except for eight chairs and one stool. The stool, for the BAILIFF, is downstage right. The witness chair is center stage, with the two chairs for ANASTASIA and for her attorney to the right of it. To the left, are five chairs for the defendants and their attorney. [Although there are five defendants, there are only four chairs for them. This is intentional.]
Curtain up: MARIE enters and begins to run the lines spoken by the BAILIFF at the top of the show. MARIE is a longtime, grassroots political activist, a militant feminist, and all-around uplifter-of-the-masses. All of the actors are wearing black, in preparation for the evening's performance.)

MARIE. *(Speaking as if to an audience.)* Good evening. Welcome to the Court of Women. I'm the Bailiff, and this ... *(Indicating the stage.)* is our courtroom.

(Suddenly BETTY enters. She is a theater technician, otherwise known as a stagehand, who has been pressed into service as an actor. BETTY is a butch woman of the type rarely seen on the stage of a mainstream theater. She begins to follow MARIE, repeating her lines and imitating her gestures.)

BETTY. Good evening. Welcome to the Court of Women. I'm the Bailiff, and this is our courtroom....
MARIE. *(Glancing at BETTY.)* This chair is for the plaintiff, Anastasia, and this chair is for her attorney....

BETTY. This chair is for the plaintiff, Anastasia, and this chair is for her attorney....

MARIE. *(Clearing her throat.)* Over here are the chairs for the five defendants, and ....

BETTY. Over here are the chairs for the five defendants, and ....

MARIE. *(Very rapidly.)* And here is the chair for the defense attorney. Now, you'll notice there's no judge's bench or jury box—

BETTY. *(Matching her tempo.)* And here is the chair for the defense attorney. Now, you'll notice there's no judge's bench or jury box—

(MARIE sits, folds her arms, and stares at BETTY.)

MARIE. Are you through?

BETTY. Yes.

MARIE. *(Rising, she resumes her monologue.)* That is because this is the Women's Court, and in the Women's Court ....

BETTY. That is because this is the Women's Court, and in the Women's Court ....

MARIE. *(Turning.)* Betty, what are you doing?

BETTY. *(Also turning.)* Betty, what are you doing?

MARIE. Betty!

BETTY. Betty! Oh ... I was ... just imitating you.

MARIE. Why?

BETTY. That was the Bailiff's part, wasn't it?

MARIE. You mean you don't know?

BETTY. I can't remember anything!

MARIE. Well, maybe you won't get the Bailiff's part tonight.

BETTY. I don't want any of the parts!

MARIE. Betty, how can you say that?

BETTY. It's easy. I'm not an actor. I'm a stagehand.

MARIE. But you know in the Emma Goldman Theater Brigade we don't observe hierarchy.

BETTY. What does that have to do with making me act when I don't want to?

MARIE. This isn't about *making* you act, Betty. It's about equal opportunity. It's the only way we can break out of the class structure of traditional theater.

BETTY. Why can't I just run lights, if that's what I want to do?

MARIE. Because, Betty, when you say, "That's what I want to do," what you really mean is, "That's what I've been *conditioned* to want to do."

BETTY. But I hate being out here.

MARIE. Why?

BETTY. Because it's uncomfortable.

MARIE. Exactly! It's "uncomfortable." It's uncomfortable, because it's unfamiliar. And that is no accident. Think, Betty—Why is it that some women are less comfortable in the limelight? Because they don't conform to the patriarchal stereotypes about women! And why do you think some women are right at home in the spotlight? Because they grew up white and middle class, and their parents could afford to get their teeth straightened! Because they grew up believing they were naturally *entitled*! Don't you see, Betty, that what you feel comfortable with is not a choice at all, but a culturally conditioned response. It is the goal of the Emma Goldman Theater Brigade to break down the walls of these artificially imposed barriers between women and to liberate the spirit within all of us that transcends class and race and looks and age and physical ability.... The Emma Goldman Theater Brigade is smashing centuries of oppressive tradition in the theater—

BETTY. *(Cutting her off.)* But we're supposed to memorize all the parts in the whole play!

MARIE. *(Exasperated.)* Well, of course, Betty. That's because the only way to be sure the casting is fair, is to use a lottery system every night, and the only way to use a lottery system is for all the actors to know all the parts.

BETTY. But I can't remember any lines.

MARIE. You did beautifully last night at dress rehearsal.

BETTY. But last night I was Anastasia, and she hasn't got any lines!

MARIE. Well, maybe you'll get lucky and draw her again tonight.

BETTY. Look, I've been thinking about this thing. There's nine parts in the show, right? And so that's nine chances to one that I might draw any particular part, right? But, see, now that's changed, because last night I drew Anastasia, so now the odds of me drawing that same name two nights in a row are eighty-one to one, right? So, you see, I have a worse chance of getting her part tonight than you do, or anyone else, because no one else will be drawing it twice in a row, see? So, you see, I don't have an equal chance anymore. So I'm being discriminated against.

MARIE. No, you're not. Diane brings the hat out. She mixes up the names. We all draw one. The hat doesn't know you drew Anastasia last night. The slips of paper don't know you drew Anastasia last night. Perfect equality.

(DONNA enters. DONNA is one of those actors whose talent is eclipsed by her perpetual paranoia that someone else—in this case, the director of the company—is standing in her light.)

DONNA. "Perfect equality!" I bet Diane draws one of the attorneys' parts tonight.

MARIE. She has the same chance as the rest of us.

BETTY. *(Crossing to the upstage right chair.)* Except for me....

DONNA. *(To MARIE.)* Oh, come on. She probably takes out the slip she wants before she passes the hat.

MARIE. What makes you say that?

DONNA. She's a complete and total control freak. Can you really see her settling on opening night for the role of Anastasia? The great Diane Anthony, founder and director of the revolutionary

Theater Brigade? Can you really see her drawing a non-speaking role?

MARIE. The lottery was her idea!

DONNA. What better way to disguise the mechanics of her dictatorship than with a dramatic display of democracy. Brings tears to your eyes, doesn't it, the thought of her coming down among the ranks of the lowly actors to play Russian roulette with the casting?

MARIE. Diane did not found this theater to forward her career, believe me. If that was her aim, she'd be working in the mainstream instead of some small, political, women's theater.

DONNA. And that's why she just happens to be the head of the company.

MARIE. She just happens to be the head of the company, because she does ninety-nine percent of the work, or hadn't you noticed?

DONNA. I notice that every time someone else comes up with an idea, everyone has to ask Diane about it.

MARIE. Well, maybe because Diane is the only one in the company whose vision transcends personality.

DONNA. You just see. She's going to pull one of the attorney's roles tonight.

MARIE. Well, then why don't *you* pass the hat?

BETTY. *(Suddenly galvanized, she crosses to DONNA.)* Yes! *You* pass it! Here!—Here's five dollars. No, here's twenty. You take Anastasia's name out of the hat before we draw, and give it to me! *(Dropping to her knees.)* Please, please, please, please....

(MELISSA has entered during BETTY's speech. MELISSA is not the sharpest pencil in the box—probably one of the reasons she puts so much stock in the opinions of the critics.)

MELISSA. *(Eyeing the money suspiciously.)* What's going on? Betty, what are you doing?

BETTY. *(Busted.)* I was just ....

DONNA. She was getting into character.

MELISSA. Which one?

BETTY. Anastasia.

MELISSA. What makes you think you'll get Anastasia?

BETTY. *(Too quickly.)* Nothing. In fact, I probably won't.

MELISSA. What are you doing with this money?

BETTY. I ... uh ....

DONNA. She was trying to see how it would feel to be Anastasia and lose all her money. *(Taking the money.)* There! And you'll never get any of it back. How does that make you feel, Betty?

BETTY. Pretty pissed off.

DONNA. Good. *(To MELISSA.)* She's very serious about her acting.

MELISSA. Good thing, because I just checked the reservation list, and *both* critics are going to be here tonight.

BETTY. No!

DONNA. Really? They've never come to our shows before. I wonder what made them decide—

MELISSA. Well, all I know is their names are on the list, and I hope I get one of the good parts.

MARIE. They're all good.

MELISSA. Only some are more good than others.

(ATHENA enters. She is the daughter of a wealthy man, the epitome of entitlement. Her arrogance masks her abysmal ignorance about the world outside her ivory tower, and she's too smart not to be suspecting as much.)

ATHENA. Has anybody seen our celebrated playwright?

MELISSA. Athena, guess what? The critics are going to be here tonight ... both of them!

ATHENA. I know. I sent them the tickets.

MARIE. *(Rising to confront her nemesis.)* You what?

ATHENA. *(Relishing another opportunity to yank MARIE's chain.)* I sent them comp tickets and a brief, but flattering note.

BAILIFF. No!

MARIE. And who told you to do that?

ATHENA. No one. I thought it would be good publicity for us to get reviewed.

MARIE. Athena, I don't like that you did that without consulting the company.

MELISSA. Why? I'm glad they're coming.

MARIE. Because we don't care what the patriarchy thinks of our theater.

ATHENA. But we should make use of "the patriarchy" any time we can get it to serve our interests.

MARIE. No! Wrong! Don't you know that's been the excuse behind women's collaboration with men and our betrayal of each other for two thousand years? Don't you know that the idea of working within the system for change has been the biggest boondoggle in the history of women's oppression? That's exactly the kind of argument that has kept us from having our own theaters and taking our own culture seriously!

MELISSA. If it bothers you, don't read the reviews.

MARIE. That's not the point!

MELISSA. Well, what is?

MARIE. Inviting the male gaze!

ATHENA and MELISSA. *(Turning toward each other in mock terror.)* Ooo … "the male gaze…!"

MARIE. *(Soldiering on.)* We have been so trained to see ourselves through their eyes—

ATHENA. *(Smiling.)* Speak for yourself.

MARIE. Have a good laugh, but the joke's on you. *(To MELISSA.)* You can spend your life hanging on the words of male critics … *(To ATHENA.)* … or going to law school to study how to be just like them, but when all is said and done, who's going to give you your identity?

MELISSA. *(To ATHENA.)* My god—that sounds just like a play I once did. Little political thing in one of those women's theater companies. What was it called?

ATHENA. *The Anastasia Trials in the Court of Women?*

MELISSA. How did you know? Did you see it?

ATHENA. No, but I read the reviews.

MARIE. *(Crossing down left again.)* Oh, shut up.

(Just then DIANE and LISA enter. They are conferring over script changes. DIANE is the head of the company. She is passionate about her mission to produce feminist theater, and she naively and mistakenly assumes the other members of the company share her vision. Ignoring the petty jealousies and personal agendas that are tearing the company apart, she remains blissfully ignorant of the impending train wreck. LISA, the playwright, is like DIANE in that her commitment to feminism does not incorporate any practical engagement with actual women. She deeply resents the fact that her works of art are dependent on the caprices of these flawed creatures for their actualization.)

ATHENA. *(Turning.)* Ah, the playwright. Just who I wanted to see.

LISA. *(Looking up from her rewrites.)* What?

MELISSA. *(To DIANE.)* Diane, did you see the list of reservations?

DIANE. *(To MELISSA.)* No, why?

MELISSA. The critics are coming! Both of them!

DIANE. *(To MELISSA.)* That's nice. *(To the other actors.)* Look, is everyone here yet?

DONNA. *(To MARIE.)* You see?

MARIE. *(To DONNA.)* See what?

DONNA. How casual she was...."That's nice." Like she doesn't care.

MARIE. She doesn't.

DONNA. Oh, right.

ATHENA. *(To LISA.)* I wanted to talk to you about some changes in the script.

BETTY. What? No! No changes!

LISA. *(Threatened by ATHENA's education and privilege.)* We open in a few minutes.

ATHENA. But these are important. The play isn't going to make sense—

DIANE. *(Calling out.)* Look! Is everyone here?

LISA. *(To ATHENA.)* It's too late.

ATHENA. *(To LISA.)* But if anyone in the audience knows anything about the law—

LISA. I'm not a lawyer— I'm a playwright.

ATHENA. But it's about a trial.

LISA. In the *Women's* Court—a whole different paradigm.

DIANE. *(To the company.)* Okay, listen! Who's *not* here?

JENNY. *(An offstage wail.)* Me! *(She enters. JENNY is a perpetual hypochondriac. This is her way of deflecting criticism, while garnering support for her fragile talent.)* I'm not here....

DONNA. *(Defender of the weak.)* What's the matter, hon?

JENNY. I'm sick. *(Expressions of sympathy: "Oh, that's too bad." "I'm sorry...," etc.)* I don't think I can go on. *(Sudden shift in climate: "Oh, sure you can." "You're not that sick." "You have to," etc.)* Diane, I can't...

DONNA. Why are you telling Diane? This is a collective.

JENNY. *(Staggering across the stage.)* I went to bed with this headache last night, and then in the middle of the night, I woke up and I started vomiting, and I've been vomiting all day. I had to pull over twice on the way to the theater. Only I haven't eaten all day, so it's not really solid. It's this kind of green, watery—

(JENNY lies down across the defendants' chairs.)

MELISSA. We can't cancel the show! The critics are going to be here!

MARIE. Screw the critics!

DONNA. I know! Why don't we let her play Annie Jennings tonight? Annie only comes on at the end of the second act. That way she could lie down, or vomit, or whatever, until the play's almost over. Shed just have to come on at the very end. And by then, she might be better.

MARIE. But what about the lottery?

DONNA. The whole point of the lottery was to empower the actors. I don't see how it's going to empower us to have an actor throw up in the middle of her lines.

BETTY. Yes! Yes! Exactly! Yes! *(To MARIE.)* Yes! Yes! You see?

LISA. *(Standing on the witness chair.)* Excuse me.... Excuse me....

DIANE. Hey, could we have some quiet, please? Our playwright has something to say!

LISA. I added a character last night—

(A riot ensues.)

DIANE. *(Yelling.)* Will you let her finish, please?

LISA. I added the character of Zinaida in the first act—

(More rioting.)

DIANE. *Please!*

LISA. I added the character of Zinaida in the first act, and so the actor playing Annie in the second act, will have to double as this new character Zinaida—

BETTY. The lines! The lines!

DIANE. Listen!

LISA. So, since nobody's had the chance to learn Zinaida's lines—

BETTY. How could we? We've never seen them!

LISA. I'm going to have to play the part—and the part of Annie tonight. Which is why we can't give Annie's part to anyone.

MARIE. Wait a minute! Wait a minute! I don't like what I'm hearing. *(To DIANE.)* You mean after all those months of meetings to come up with a system of casting that's fair to everyone—we're just going to throw it out the window?

MELISSA. Oh, for Pete's sake! We're just going to let one woman play one role for one night, because of special circumstances.

BETTY. Special circumstances—yes! *(To MARIE.)* You see? Special circumstances!

MARIE. What special circumstances? Who is this Zinaida character? We've been doing fine without her. Why do we have to have her now?

MELISSA. Oh, who cares? It's ten minutes to curtain. Let's draw the parts so we can have a chance to look over our lines. They're going to review the performance tonight.

JENNY. *(Sitting up at the mention of getting reviewed.)* Ohhh ....

MARIE. I don't care if we hold up the curtain or if we have to send the audience home. I agreed to do this play with a lottery system, and here it is opening night—and what do we see? Good old boys, special privileges, and—as usual—the need to set aside our principles for the sake of some internally manufactured crisis.

JENNY. *(Indignant.)* Is she talking about my diarrhea?

ATHENA. *(To DIANE.)* I have a question.

DIANE. What?

ATHENA. *(Addressing DIANE.)* If the playwright is adding a character, is that character going to take the stand?

LISA. Yes.

ATHENA. *(To DIANE.)* Then won't the Bailiff and the attorneys need extra lines?

BETTY. No! No!

LISA. *(Holding up the rewrites.)* I've written those down, so the actors can just carry them on like they're legal papers, and then they can refer to them when it comes to that part of the script. It's very simple.

DONNA. There's nothing simple about this play. It's the most complicated show I've ever done.

BETTY. Me too!

MELISSA. *(To DIANE.)* Yeah, you know when you said we were doing a play about Anastasia, I was thinking it would be like that movie with Ingrid Bergman.

JENNY. *(Forgetting to be sick.)* I saw that! And Yul Brynner.

MELISSA. Only he was wearing a toupee.

JENNY. I think it was his real hair. He wasn't really bald.

LISA. That movie was a fairy tale! The story of the real Anastasia had nothing to do with romance. It was a story of oppression and betrayal.

MELISSA. What's wrong with romance? People like love stories.

LISA. Oh, sure—especially women. They're riding to work right now, as we speak, all over the world, clutching a regency novel in one hand and a subway strap in the other, on their way to some boring, demeaning job that only women can learn to tolerate, that barely pays them enough to cover rent and groceries—and of course, their weekly fix of cheap romance. Either that, or they're riding home to their emotionally-absent, parasitic, or tyrannical husbands and families. But none of this matters as long as Cecily Hargrave can manage to flash those defiant eyes at the arrogant Lord Beaverbrook as Count Twickendick hands her into his coach for the masquerade ball. Women love romance. Sure. That's why they betray women like Anastasia. Because they'll believe in romance even if it kills them.

MARIE. That's right! Going through life addicted to romance, women squander their capacity for radical action on the cheap baubles of patriarchy!

MELISSA. Well, excuse me for living! I'm going to get the hat.

ATHENA. *(To DIANE.)* I have something to say about this script. I'm in law school—

LISA. Where they teach you to write plays?

ATHENA. Diane?

DONNA. Stop talking to her! She's not our mother!

ATHENA. *(To DIANE.)* This play is full of legal mistakes—

LISA. Arrest me.

ATHENA. *(Still to DIANE.)* And I think this business of adding a witness that nobody's ever seen before—

LISA. *I'll* play her part. It won't be a problem.

MARIE. *(To DIANE.)* I agree with Athena. I feel the playwright has taken a lot of our power by changing—

LISA. *(Stung by MARIE's defection.)* I made it better! Do you hear? This is a better play! I'm sorry I couldn't call you all up last night and read it to you in the middle of the night, but my ideas don't even wait for my permission. You think I enjoyed typing all night?

MARIE. So, in other words, you're not accountable for your actions?

LISA. *(To DIANE, beginning to cry.)* It's impossible. I can't work like this…. I don't know what these people want. I give them my blood, my tears, my guts….

JENNY. *(Remembering that she's sick.)* Ohhh….

DIANE. All right…. Now, listen! This is an important play on an important subject. *(To LISA.)* It's a beautiful play. *(To the troops.)* Tonight is the world premiere. We've all worked very hard. We've all learned all the parts in the play, just so that we can be absolutely fair and equal with each other, and we're all working together for the same thing: the empowerment of women. And we have a playwright here who was up all night making sure that the play would be the very best that it could be, and we can respond to her integrity and her discipline by showing her our appreciation.

(DIANE applauds. BETTY starts to clap, but stops when she realizes that none of the other actors are applauding.)

MARIE. Sounds to me like the playwright has power over the actors.

DIANE. *(To MARIE.)* The *play*. The play has power over the actors … *(Appealing to the other actors.)* … and the actors have power over the play. Please … we have enough real enemies out there. We don't need to make enemies of each other.

MELISSA. *(Arriving with the hat, she hands it to DIANE.)* Let's go, let's go! We've got five minutes!

DONNA. *I'll* pass the hat. *(She snatches it out of DIANE's hands.)* You passed it last night. This is a collective.

JENNY. What about me?

LISA. *(To DIANE.)* If she doesn't go on, we won't be able to do the play.

DONNA. Give her Anastasia. If she throws up, it'll be in character.

BETTY. No! Not Anastasia. *(She nudges DONNA to remind her of their deal. DONNA stares back at her as if BETTY's crazy. Desperate, BETTY turns back to the others.)* Besides, anybody can vomit. You just stick your fingers down your throat.

(She starts to demonstrate.)

JENNY. *(Not to be upstaged.)* Oh, god ….

MARIE. *(Slapping BETTY's hand.)* Betty, stop that! Here, draw!

BETTY. First? I can't go first!

MELISSA. *(Suspicious.)* Why not?

BETTY. *(Thinking fast.)* Because … I went first last night! *(To the company.)* This is a collective. I'll go last ….

(She nudges DONNA again, but DONNA continues to ignore her.)

DIANE. Wait! Let me take Annie's name out, since we already know who's going to play it.

DONNA. *I'll* take it out.

(She grabs the hat away from DIANE. Just then AMY enters. AMY is an actor who has what might be considered "sex appeal" in

mainstream theater, and she makes the most of it. To AMY, women's theater is like staying home with your girlfriend on prom night, and she can't wait to get out.)

AMY. So, what is this? The lottery without me? What's going on?

DIANE. I'm sorry. We thought everyone was here.

DONNA. *Diane* thought.

AMY. Oh, sure, I'm going to believe that. Just like I'm going to believe it's the luck of the draw that Anastasia is going to just happen to be the last name in the hat.

BETTY. *(Delighted.)* It is? *(Oops.)* I mean, if it was, it would be pure coincidence. Well ... eighty-one to one, actually ....

DONNA. *(Handing LISA the slip with "Annie Jennings" on it.)* Okay, here's yours.... Now, let's draw.

AMY. Wait a minute! Not so fast! I saw that! What's with giving the name to her? Aren't we supposed to draw?

DONNA. Show up on time and maybe you'd catch a clue.

AMY. Hey, fuck you. My bus was late. *(To LISA.)* Let me see.

(She grabs the slip of paper.)

DIANE. There were some changes to the script—

AMY. *(Ignoring DIANE, she reads.)* Oh—"Annie Jennings." Who wants her anyway? *(To LISA.)* You can have her every night. In fact, if I ever draw her, I'll give her to you.

MARIE. *(Disgusted.)* Look, I'm drawing from the hat! Anyone else want to know who they're playing tonight?

(The actors become quiet as the hat goes around. JENNY is the next to the last to draw. BETTY goes to take the hat from her, but she snatches it back and vomits into it.)

JENNY. Sorry.

BETTY. Now what am I going to do? I can't draw!

DIANE. *(Retrieving the hat.)* Okay, let's all say what we drew so we can figure out Betty's part by process of elimination.

ATHENA. *(Aside.)* So to speak.

JENNY. Defense attorney.

(She gags and exits up left.)

MELISSA. Hey! That's the biggest part in the show! She can't play that!

DONNA. We have to let her trade with someone!

MELISSA. I'll trade with her. *(Crossing down to DIANE.)* Diane, let me trade with her!

BETTY. *(To MELISSA.)* What did you get?

MELISSA. Nurse Thea.

DONNA. *(To MELISSA.)* You just want to trade, so you can show off for the critics.

BETTY. *(To AMY.)* Who did you draw?

AMY. Baroness Sophie Buxhoeveden.

MELISSA. Lucky!

AMY. I'm not complaining.

MELISSA. *(To DIANE.)* Look, I can play the defense attorney.

DONNA. And so can I! So can all of us!

MELISSA. *(To DONNA.)* What did you get?

DONNA. Shura.

MELISSA. That's a good part.

DONNA. Oh, yeah. About as good as Nurse Thea.

BETTY. *(To MARIE.)* What did you get?

MARIE. The bag lady, Clara Peuthert.

BETTY. *(To DIANE.)* What about you, Diane?

DIANE. Prosecuting attorney.

ATHENA. Congratulations!

DONNA. Best role in the show. *(To MARIE.)* What a coincidence.

DIANE. *(To DONNA.)* What are you saying?

MELISSA. *(To DONNA.) You* passed the hat.

DONNA. But it was on Diane's makeup table, wasn't it? She had plenty of time to palm it and then fake drawing one.

BETTY. *(To ATHENA.)* So, Athena, what did you get?

ATHENA. Anastasia.

BETTY. No! I'm ruined! I'm ruined!

DIANE. That means you must be the Bailiff.

BETTY. No, no! Not the Bailiff! The Bailiff has almost as many lines as the attorneys!

MELISSA. *(To BETTY with a certain malicious glee.)* That's right. And the Bailiff talks to the audience.

BETTY. No! No! What am I going to do?

MELISSA. Want to trade?

MARIE. No! No trades! Absolutely. We've already violated the system once. That's enough.

MELISSA. *(Checking her watch in the hopes of distracting MARIE.)* Hey, it's almost curtain!

LISA. Diane, here are the rewrites for the attorneys. Where's the defense attorney?

(DIANE takes a set of papers.)

ATHENA. She's in the bathroom. Here. I'll give them to her. *(She takes the rest of the rewrites.)* Let's go! Betty's got to open the show!

BETTY. No! No!

ATHENA. *(To BETTY.)* You'll do great.

(Handing BETTY a set of rewrites.)

DIANE. Come on! Five minutes to curtain!

(The actors exit, except for AMY and MELISSA. AMY grabs MELISSA as she is about to leave.)

AMY. Can I talk to you a second?

MELISSA. Me? *(AMY has never talked to her before.)* What do you want?

AMY. *(Putting her arm around MELISSA.)* I need to ask a favor.

MELISSA. *(Staring at AMY's hand on her shoulder.)* What is it?

AMY. *(Backing off.)* I need to leave after intermission, and I want you to tell the others I got sick.

MELISSA. You're leaving the theater?

(Just then ATHENA enters, carrying ANASTASIA's coat. She hides behind a curtain to overhear what's going on.)

AMY. Yeah. It's one of those things—I got this booking a couple of months ago—before I got in the play——and I forgot all about it. When I remembered, I tried to get out of it—

MELISSA. You're in another show?

AMY. It's a cabaret spot at the Eastland Hotel [or name of local upscale nightclub].

MELISSA. A nightclub act?

AMY. Yeah.

MELISSA. And you *forgot* you had the booking? *(AMY shrugs.)* You mean you're going to walk out on the play just because of some nightclub gig?

AMY. I have to. They're paying me…

MELISSA. *(This changes everything.)* They're paying you…?

AMY. *(Examining her nails.)* Three hundred bucks.

MELISSA. I can't believe it!

(MELISSA crosses to her new buddy, but AMY rises in alarm and crosses away from her.)

AMY. I don't care what you believe. You're lucky I showed up at all! I wasn't going to, but since some of the parts are only in the first act, I decided to come and see what I got. And Sophie is in the first act....

MELISSA. But the critics are going to be here!

AMY. This is women's theater. They're not going to get it anyway. Look—do me this favor and tell them I'm sick, and I'll let you trade roles with me for the rest of the run.

MELISSA. But we can't.

AMY. Sure we can. Stand next to me when we draw, and if you like what I have, it's yours. *(She tries the arm-around-the-shoulder again.)* What do you say?

MELISSA. Okay.... *(Mission accomplished, AMY turns to go.)* But you're going to be here for the rest of the shows, aren't you?

AMY. *(Already gone.)* So far.

(MELISSA exits. JENNY wanders back on, and ATHENA emerges from her hiding place.)

JENNY. Where did everyone go?

ATHENA. They're changing. It's almost curtain.

JENNY. Oh, shit! I've got to put on all those lawyer clothes....

(She starts to exit, but ATHENA stops her.)

ATHENA. You don't have to be the attorney.

JENNY. *(Turning.)* I don't?

ATHENA. No. We decided you were too sick.

JENNY. But I thought everyone—

ATHENA. We decided it wasn't fair to make you carry such a big role when you were feeling so sick.

JENNY. *(A long pause as she notices the coat ATHENA is carrying.)* So who am I?

ATHENA. Anastasia.

JENNY. *(Nodding.)* Oh.

ATHENA. You won't have to say anything.

JENNY. *(A long pause.)* I know I'm too sick to do a good job as the attorney, but there's a part of me that was excited about doing it anyway. I'll probably never draw it again. *(ATHENA doesn't say anything.)* Well—I guess it's better for me to be Anastasia ... better for the company.

ATHENA. I brought you your costume, so you can change in the wings and not have to put up with all the craziness in the dressing room.

JENNY. Thanks, Athena. That was really thoughtful.

ATHENA. No problem.

JENNY. Who's going to play the defense attorney?

ATHENA. I am.

JENNY. *(Another long pause.)* Well, you'll probably do a better job than I would.

ATHENA. Who knows? Have a good show.

(JENNY exits up left. ATHENA takes a proprietary look around the stage and exits up left also. Blackout. The lights come up on an empty stage. Whispers are heard off right: "Where's Betty?" Betty! "Betty!" etc. The lights go out again and come up again.)

BETTY. *(Offstage.)* No, oh, no, please, oh, please.... *(BETTY is pushed on stage from up right. She turns and exits immediately. BETTY wears a BAILIFF's shirt. She has a copy of the script stuffed in her back pocket.)* No! No!

(Offstage voices are heard: "Go on!" "Get out there!" etc. BETTY is pushed on stage again. This time she looks up at the audience and freezes, a deer trapped in headlights. Finally, someone offstage whispers the first line of the play, "Good evening." BETTY turns to stare into the wings at the speaker. The line is repeated. BETTY turns woodenly toward the audience.)

BETTY/BAILIFF. Good evening. *(Turning back toward the*

wings for her next line.) Welcome to the Court of Women. *(To her prompter in the wings.)* That's it. That's all I remember. *(To the audience.)* Look, I don't know any of my lines, and that's going to be a real problem for both of us. *(Something from the wings.)* What? Oh. Really? That's okay? *(To the audience.)* Okay. So I don't know my lines, but I have a general idea what they say, and so I'm just going to tell you what I do remember, and that's going to have to do for tonight. But if you take a rain check, the odds are eighty-one to one that someone else is going to be the Bailiff for the next show.... *(Noise from wings.)* What? Oh. *(To audience.)* I wasn't supposed to say that. So, okay. Let's see. I'm the Bailiff, and this is our courtroom. This is where Anastasia is going to sit, with her attorney ...here. She's the plaintiff. And then these chairs are all for the defendants. There's five of them, only one of them is going to be somebody else until the second act, which is probably going to be confusing, but you might as well get used to that, because it's a pretty confusing play. *(Noise from the wings.)* Hey, get off my ass! I'm doing fine. Everybody's a critic. *(To the audience.)* Where was I? The courtroom. Oh, yeah. And here's the witness chair.... And you'll notice there isn't any place for the judge to sit, which is on purpose, because there isn't any judge. The playwright told us that was because in the Court of Women every woman is the judge, but I got my own idea about it. *(Noise from the wings. BETTY turns upstage.)* What's wrong with that? Why is the playwright's opinion more valuable than mine? *(To the audience.)* See, from the actor's point of view, the role of a judge would be kind of a problem, because we're all rotating the parts every night, so if I drew the part of the judge, I would end up having to pass a judgment on the character I played the night before— see? And nobody wants to judge themselves, or the person they used to be, or might be in the future, because at the next lottery, I could always draw the person I condemned the night before. See? So, good riddance to the judge. Okay, but here's the catch, see—You can't have a trial without a verdict, right? What's the point? So, you're going to be the judge and the jury. Yeah, that's right. Dirty trick, isn't it? We advertise a play, and then *you* pay *us* money, and then after you get here, we tell you you're the jury. Yeah, I'd be pissed, too. *(Noise from the wings.)* Audiences have rights, too, you know. *(To the audience.)* So, we've got to keep things moving. We're running a little late tonight. Even for a women's theater company. *(Protest from the wings.)* It was a joke! *(To the audience.)* So, like I was saying … you're the jury. And that's no big deal, because all you have to do is have an opinion. Like you don't already, even though we haven't started yet. *(Noise from the wings.)* Can't I say anything? *(To the audience.)* How am I doing? Am I doing okay? Just clap, if I'm doing okay. Come on! *(Let's hope they clap.)* Thank you. See if anyone else gets a private ovation tonight. Okay, and one last thing I have to tell you. Since we haven't got a judge, you people are going to have to rule on the motions, which means that every time one of the lawyers pops up with "I object," you have to decide whether or not to sustain it or overrule it. And this is really easy, don't worry. You all have those red and green cards, like traffic lights, right? Okay. Well, I'll call for the motion, and then, if you want to stop what's going on, you hold up the red card, or if you think what's going on is just fine and should keep on going, you hold up the green card. See? Simple. Like traffic lights—stop and go, right? So, let's practice. *(Anticipating trouble from the wings.)* Hey, they've never done it before. *(To audience.)* So, one of the attorneys yells "Objection!" If you want to keep *going*, what do you do? *(They hold up the green cards.)* Great. Beautiful. And now the attorney yells "Objection," and you want to *stop* what's going on. What do you do? *(They hold up red cards.)* See? Easy. *(To the wings.)* No problem. *(To the audience.)* Oh—here comes Anastasia and her attorney, Diane. Guess you don't need me anymore.

(BETTY crosses to the stool and sits. She starts to study a script. JENNY enters from up left, and DIANE enters from up right. They meet in the center, and DIANE escorts JENNY to the downstage right chair. JENNY wears a long black coat, buttoned

up over her head. DIANE is dressed as the PROSECUTING ATTORNEY. She carries her rewrites and puts them under her chair. JENNY and DIANE sit. DONNA, MARIE, MELISSA, and AMY file in from up right and sit in the chairs for the defendants. MARIE wears a tattered shawl and carries several battered shopping bags. DONNA wears a woman's hat from the 1920's, AMY wears a fur stole and diamond jewelry, and MELISSA wears a nurse's cap. After they are seated, ATHENA, dressed as the DEFENSE ATTORNEY, enters from up left, carrying her rewrites. DIANE reacts violently to the sight of ATHENA.)

DIANE. Athena? What are you doing?

ATHENA/DEFENSE ATTORNEY. Defending my clients.

DIANE. But you're supposed to be Anastasia. Who's this? *(DIANE opens the coat to look at her client. To JENNY.)* You're supposed to be the defense attorney!

JENNY. But Athena told me you all decided—

ATHENA/DEFENSE ATTORNEY. *(Cutting JENNY off, she addresses DIANE.)* Do you need some time to consult with your client?

DIANE/PROSECUTING ATTORNEY. *(After a long look at ATHENA.)* No, I think I understand her case perfectly.

JENNY. You mean I wasn't supposed to trade?

ATHENA/DEFENSE ATTORNEY. Bailiff ... you have a line, I believe.

(She sits, putting her rewrites under her chair.)

BETTY/BAILIFF. *(Rising.)* Oh! *(She checks her script.)* All rise. *(The actors rise. If the audience has not risen, BETTY repeats the line: "I said, All rise.")* The Women's Court is now in session. You can sit down.

(Audience sits, and DIANE rises to address them.)

DIANA/PROSECUTING ATTORNEY. Good evening, women of the jury ... and sisters. Tonight you're going to hear a case about a woman who was denied her identity—denied it by women she loved, women she trusted, women she depended on. And you can see all too well the tragic consequences of these betrayals.... *(She indicates JENNY, who is under the coat.)* This woman you see now, cowering under her coat, has not been allowed to be who she is. This woman, members of the jury, this woman you see next to me, was once one of the most celebrated women in Europe, the Grand Duchess Anastasia Nicolaievna Romanov, daughter of the Tsar of Russia. But that life ended tragically for her on the night of July 16, 1918, when she was ripped from her bed, led with the other members of her family into a dark courtyard of their Siberian prison, and forced to witness the brutal massacre of her entire family. There, in that terrible courtyard, this girl—and girl she was, for she was only seventeen at the time — would have also been murdered, had it not been for the fact that she lost consciousness and the body of her sister Tatiana fell on top of her, shielding her from the worst of the bayonet lances that followed the shooting. Rescued by a soldier who had been ordered to bury the bodies, suffering a smashed jaw and bayonet wounds, she was smuggled out of Russia in a hay cart, delirious with fever, to spend two years in hiding before perilously making her way to Berlin, where she attempted to end her life by jumping into the Landwehr Canal on February 17, 1920. Refusing to give her name to the police who rescued her, she was considered insane and sent to a Dalldorf public mental asylum, where she spent another two years, suffering in silence. Finally, in 1922, she told her secret and her painful ordeal should have ended. This heroic martyr should have been restored to her title, she should have come into the legacy left for her as the only surviving member of the Russian imperial family. She should have been welcomed and honored by the relatives of her family and the entire community of Russian emigrants who had fled the Revolution. She should have been able to rest, to heal from her horrendous experiences. But this did not happen. She was denied, slandered, rejected, ridiculed, libeled, cheated, and abandoned. This woman, that you see before you today, was denied her identity and her heritage by other women ... *(Turning toward the defendants.)* ... women who were motivated by greed, jealousy, and sadism ... *(Turning to JENNY.)* ... women who abused her *because* she was a survivor. *(Confronting the audience.)* And how many of you have known the special torment of being denied your identity by *other women*? Few of us have recourse to a public trial, but tonight, right here, this woman is going to have her day in court. This is a miracle, sisters, a miracle of justice in an unjust world. This woman is going to be given a hearing, sisters, a *fair* hearing, because you are going to give it to her. I ask you to hear this case as if you were standing in the shoes of my client, as if you yourself were this woman who has been so brutalized by her experiences, so tortured by her betrayers, that she is beyond the reach of traditional therapies. Without justice, sisters, there is no healing for this woman. And so I ask you to stand in her shoes to hear this case, because this woman you see next to me, cringing in terror, could have been—and might still be—any one of you!

(DIANE sits.)

ATHENA/DEFENSE ATTORNEY. *(Rising.)* Women of the jury.... You have just heard a very eloquent plea from my esteemed colleague—a plea to render justice to this unfortunate woman by turning in a verdict of "guilty" against these five women. I want to assure you that I want justice for this woman as much as my colleague does. She has certainly been the victim of a terrible fate, and her suffering is obvious to all of us. I am not here to argue that. And I want to see justice done today, but, women of the jury, a verdict of "guilty" will not bring that justice! It will not restore this woman's health. It will not give her back the lost years. It will not recover her lost inheritance. It will not do any of these things. But what it will do is turn five innocent women into scapegoats, convicted criminals. And it will do something else. If my clients are found guilty, there will be a legal precedent set for thousands of lawsuits all over the world—lawsuits of women against women. It is my intention to prove that every woman is responsible for her own identity. It is my intention to demonstrate that this is not a perfect world, that women must compete to survive, that women are not above the laws of nature, and that our justice system exists to mediate the disputes caused by this imperfect world, *not* to impose a utopian social order—as my colleague seems to think! This mythology of sisterhood is tearing women apart. It is destroying our ability to act independently in our own best interests. It is keeping us locked in patterns of dependence and submission. Women of the jury, it is a grave mistake to believe that holding each other to some mythical standard of perfection is going to bring us any closer to justice. And if you attempt to impose this myth of sisterhood, you will end by creating a reign of terror.

(ATHENA sits. There is a long pause. DIANE turns to look at BETTY.)

BETTY/BAILIFF. *(Rising with a jolt.)* Oh! I call … *(Checking her script.)* … Thea Malinowsky to the stand. *(MELISSA rises and crosses to the witness chair and BETTY crosses to swear her in.)* State your name.

MELISSA/THEA MALINOWSKY. Thea Malinowsky.

BETTY/BAILIFF. Do you swear to tell the truth, the whole truth, and nothing but the truth?

MELISSA/THEA MALINOWSKY. I do.

(BETTY returns to her stool and DIANE rises.)

DIANE/PROSECUTING ATTORNEY. Thea, what do you do?

MELISSA/THEA MALINOWSKY. I work as a nurse at the Dalldorf Mental Asylum.

DIANE/PROSECUTING ATTORNEY. Will you state your connection to the plaintiff?

MELISSA/THEA MALINOWSKY. Anastasia—I mean, the

Grand Duchess—

DIANE/PROSECUTING ATTORNEY. *(Pointedly.)* You may call her Anastasia. That's her name.

MELISSA/THEA MALINOWSKY. Anastasia was a patient at Dalldorf when I started working there. I was a night nurse on her ward.

DIANE/PROSECUTING ATTORNEY. And so you knew who she was?

MELISSA/THEA MALINOWSKY. Well, no. I mean, I knew her as Fraulein Unbekannt. That's what we called her. Nobody knew who she really was.

DIANE/PROSECUTING ATTORNEY. So you called her "Miss Unknown?"

MELISSA/THEA MALINOWSKY. Yes.

DIANE/PROSECUTING ATTORNEY. That doesn't seem very respectful or very therapeutic does it?

ATHENA/DEFENSE ATTORNEY. *(Rising.)* Objection.

BETTY/BAILIFF. *(Rising, to the audience.)* Okay, here we go....

DIANE/PROSECUTING ATTORNEY. I withdraw the question.

BETTY/BAILIFF. *(Returning to her stool.)* Off the hook this time.

(ATHENA sits.)

DIANE/PROSECUTING ATTORNEY. *(To MELISSA.)* Would you like to be called "Miss Unknown?"

MELISSA/THEA MALINOWSKY. She wouldn't tell us her name!

DIANE/PROSECUTING ATTORNEY. Please just answer the question. Would you like to be called as "Miss Unknown?"

MELISSA/THEA MALINOWSKY. No.

DIANE/PROSECUTING ATTORNEY. And did you know of her history?

MELISSA/THEA MALINOWSKY. All I knew was that she had

been there for about a year, and that they had brought her to Dalldorf, because she had jumped off a bridge in Berlin, but she wouldn't tell anyone who she was.

DIANE/PROSECUTING ATTORNEY. But she did tell someone, didn't she? She told you, didn't she?

MELISSA/THEA MALINOWSKY. Yes.

DIANE/PROSECUTING ATTORNEY. And how did she do that?

MELISSA/THEA MALINOWSKY. I was on night duty, and she came up to the desk to talk to me. She always did that with the night nurses. She never slept. She'd just come and talk all night. And this night, she had been sitting with me for about a half hour when she told me she wanted to show me something, and I asked her what it was, but she wouldn't say. I told her to bring it to me, but she wanted me to go with her to her room. And so I did, and she pulled a magazine out from under the mattress. It was a magazine she had gotten from the hospital library, and she showed it to me. She pointed to the picture on the cover and asked me if I didn't notice something special about it.

DIANE/PROSECUTING ATTORNEY. And can you tell us what it was a picture of?

MELISSA/THEA MALINOWSKY. It was a photograph of the imperial family of Russia.

DIANE/PROSECUTING ATTORNEY. Tsar Nicholas and his wife and his children?

MELISSA/THEA MALINOWSKY. Yes.

DIANE/PROSECUTING ATTORNEY. And did you notice anything special about it?

MELISSA/THEA MALINOWSKY. Not at first. I didn't know what she wanted.

DIANE/PROSECUTING ATTORNEY. But she told you to look closer, didn't she?

MELISSA/THEA MALINOWSKY. Yes.

DIANE/PROSECUTING ATTORNEY. And when you looked

closer, did you notice anything?

MELISSA/THEA MALINOWSKY. I noticed that the Tsar's youngest daughter looked a little bit like Fraulein Unbe—like Anastasia.

DIANE/PROSECUTING ATTORNEY. And did you tell her this?

MELISSA/THEA MALINOWSKY. No. I pretended I didn't see anything.

DIANE/PROSECUTING ATTORNEY. You *pretended* you didn't see anything. And can you tell the jury why you did this?

MELISSA/THEA MALINOWSKY. To test her.

DIANE/PROSECUTING ATTORNEY. To test her? And why would you want to test her?

MELISSA/THEA MALINOWSKY. Well, it was a mental asylum.

DIANE/PROSECUTING ATTORNEY. And so you lie to the patients to test them?

MELISSA/THEA MALINOWSKY. No ... I ....

DIANE/PROSECUTING ATTORNEY. You pretend you don't see things?

MELISSA/THEA MALINOWSKY. You don't—

DIANE/PROSECUTING ATTORNEY. You make them believe they are crazy, because they're supposed to be crazy anyway?

ATHENA/DEFENSE ATTORNEY. *(Rising.)* Objection. Badgering the witness.

(BETTY rises, but DIANE starts to speak.)

DIANE/PROSECUTING ATTORNEY. And so after this "test" of yours, what did the patient do?

(BETTY and ATHENA sit.)

MELISSA/THEA MALINOWSKY. She pointed to the girl in the photograph and asked me if I saw any resemblance between herself and the photo.

DIANE/PROSECUTING ATTORNEY. And did you "test" her again?

MELISSA/THEA MALINOWSKY. I admitted there was a resemblance.

DIANE/PROSECUTING ATTORNEY. Ah. And what did she do then?

MELISSA/THEA MALINOWSKY. She became very upset, and she said, "I am Her Imperial Highness the Grand Duchess Anastasia Nicolaievna."

DIANE/PROSECUTING ATTORNEY. Now, Thea, this is very important. Did you believe her?

MELISSA/THEA MALINOWSKY. I did at the time, but later—

DIANE/PROSECUTING ATTORNEY. But you did at the time. And of course, you immediately reported this to your supervisor.

MELISSA/THEA MALINOWSKY. *(Turning to her attorney for direction.)* No ....

DIANE/PROSECUTING ATTORNEY. No? You discover that the youngest daughter of the Tsar of Russia has escaped the massacre at Ekaterinburg—*(JENNY reacts to the name "Ekaterinburg" with a guttural, primal cry. DIANE has anticipated this and takes it in stride.)*...and has turned up in a mental asylum four years later in Berlin, and you don't tell your supervisor?

MELISSA/THEA MALINOWSKY. No.

DIANE/PROSECUTING ATTORNEY. This is incredible! A woman wrongfully diagnosed, wrongfully incarcerated, wrongfully separated from her family, wrongfully deprived of her inheritance— and you didn't report it to your supervisor?

MELISSA/THEA MALINOWSKY. No, I did not.

DIANE/PROSECUTING ATTORNEY. Did you report it to anyone?

MELISSA/THEA MALINOWSKY. I told my boyfriend.

DIANE/PROSECUTING ATTORNEY. Ah. Your *boyfriend.* And why did you tell him?

MELISSA/THEA MALINOWSKY. I wanted his advice.

DIANE/PROSECUTING ATTORNEY. Of course. And what did he say?

MELISSA/THEA MALINOWSKY. He laughed at me, and then he said, "What do you expect to hear at a mental asylum?"

DIANE/PROSECUTING ATTORNEY. And is that when you changed your mind about Fraulein Unbekannt's identity?

MELISSA/THEA MALINOWSKY. Yes.

DIANE/PROSECUTING ATTORNEY. No further questions.

(She crosses to her chair and sits.)

ATHENA/DEFENSE ATTORNEY. *(Rising.)* Thea, was this your first job as a nurse?

MELISSA/THEA MALINOWSKY. Yes.

ATHENA/DEFENSE ATTORNEY. And this job was very important to you, wasn't it?

DIANE/PROSECUTING ATTORNEY. *(Rising.)* Objection. Irrelevant.

ATHENA/DEFENSE ATTORNEY. Nurse Malinowsky's motives in not reporting this episode to her supervisor are precisely what she is here being tried for. I intend to establish that Nurse Malinowsky felt her job would be in jeopardy, and that this was of great concern to her.

DIANE/PROSECUTING ATTORNEY. Nurse Malinowsky's attachment to her job is irrelevant to the fact that she heard Anastasia say who she was, she believed her, and she deliberately withheld this information from those who were in a position to restore my client to her rightful identity.

BETTY/BAILIFF. *(Rising.)* Okay. Does she get to ask Thea why she needed the job? Green if she can ask her, red if she can't. *(She takes the vote and announces the result:)* Overruled [or Sustained; if Sustained, skip to *].

(BETTY and DIANE return to their seats.)

ATHENA/DEFENSE ATTORNEY. This job at Dalldorf was important to you, wasn't it?

MELISSA/THEA MALINOWSKY. Yes.

ATHENA/DEFENSE ATTORNEY. Can you tell us why it was so important?

MELISSA/THEA MALINOWSKY. I had just finished my nurses' training, and I had many debts to pay. I was also supporting my sister and her baby, because her husband had just left her.

ATHENA/DEFENSE ATTORNEY. And what would have happened to your sister if you had lost your job?

MELISSA/THEA MALINOWSKY. She would have had to give up the baby.

ATHENA/DEFENSE ATTORNEY. Thank you. And, * Nurse Malinowsky, is it your job as a nurse to diagnose the patients at Dalldorf Hospital?

DIANE/PROSECUTING ATTORNEY. *(Rising.)* Objection! Irrelevant and misleading! We are not talking about diagnosis. We are talking about identity.

ATHENA/DEFENSE ATTORNEY. I intend to prove that to the medical profession, the two are the same thing.

DIANE/PROSECUTING ATTORNEY. The medical profession is not on trial here. Thea Malinowsky, who knew who my client was and did nothing about it, is on trial.

ATHENA/DEFENSE ATTORNEY. *Nurse* Malinowsky is on trial, and I intend to prove that it was her understanding that to make the report was a violation of her job description.

BETTY/BAILIFF. *(Rising.)* Okay, can she ask Thea if nurses are supposed to diagnose? Green if she can, red if she can't. *(She takes the vote and announces the result:)* Overruled [or Sustained; if Sustained, skip to *].

(BETTY and DIANE return to their seats.)

ATHENA/DEFENSE ATTORNEY. Is it the job of the nurses to

diagnose the patients?

MELISSA/THEA MALINOWSKY. No. The doctors do that.

ATHENA/DEFENSE ATTORNEY. And if a nurse took it upon herself to diagnose the patients, what would happen to that nurse?

MELISSA/THEA MALINOWSKY. She would lose her job.

ATHENA/DEFENSE ATTORNEY. Thank you. * In your training, did they tell you what to expect when you went on the wards.

MELISSA/THEA MALINOWSKY. Yes. Our training was very thorough.

ATHENA/DEFENSE ATTORNEY. And what did they tell you to expect?

MELISSA/THEA MALINOWSKY. That many of the patients would try to convince us that they were sane, that it was all a mistake their being there. They would try to get us to believe that they were other people—secret agents, government enemies, political prisoners. They would tell us whatever they thought would get our sympathy so that we would help them get out.

ATHENA/DEFENSE ATTORNEY. They might even tell you that they were lost members of some royal family?

DIANE/PROSECUTING ATTORNEY. *(Rising.)* Objection! Leading the witness.

ATHENA/DEFENSE ATTORNEY. Withdrawn. *(DIANE sits.)* Did you think about this warning when "Fraulein Unbekannt" told you she was the Grand Duchess of Russia?

MELISSA/THEA MALINOWSKY. Yes, I did.

ATHENA/DEFENSE ATTORNEY. And this was your boyfriend's interpretation, was it not?

MELISSA/THEA MALINOWSKY. Yes.

ATHENA/DEFENSE ATTORNEY. Will you tell the jury, please, your boyfriend's occupation?

MELISSA/THEA MALINOWSKY. *(With a look of defiance at DIANE.)* He's a doctor.

ATHENA/DEFENSE ATTORNEY. Thank you. No further questions.

(ATHENA sits, and DIANE indicates that she does not want to cross-examine.)

BETTY/BAILIFF. *(Rising.)* You may step down. *(MELISSA crosses back to her chair and sits.)* Clara Peuthert to the stand. *(No one moves.)* Clara Peuthert to the stand, please.

(MARIE rises.)

MARIE/CLARA PEUTHERT. All right, all right. Don't get your panties in a wad.

(She begins to collect her numerous bags to take with her to the stand.)

ATHENA/DEFENSE ATTORNEY. You could leave those—
MARIE/CLARA PEUTHERT. The hell I could!

(She distributes her bags carefully around the witness chair.)

BETTY/BAILIFF. *(Crossing to the witness chair.)* State your name please.
MARIE/CLARA PEUTHERT. Why? You just told everybody—twice.
BETTY/BAILIFF. It's part of the swearing in.
MARIE/CLARA PEUTHERT. The swearing in? What the fucking hell is that?

(She laughs at her joke.)

BETTY/BAILIFF. Do you swear—
MARIE/CLARA PEUTHERT. Do I swear? Are you deaf?

(She laughs again.)

DIANE/PROSECUTING ATTORNEY. *(Rising.)* Clara, you are in the Court of Women. If you refuse to cooperate, you will be held in contempt of court. Do you understand?

MARIE/CLARA PEUTHERT. *(To DIANE.)* What's your name?

DIANE/PROSECUTING ATTORNEY. Diane. Are you going to cooperate?

MARIE/CLARA PEUTHERT. Diane. Let me tell you something. I have been held in contempt my whole life—my whole goddamn life Do you hear? And I'm talking *contempt. Real* contempt.

(Fishing in one of her bags for something.)

BETTY/BAILIFF. Do you swear to tell the truth, the whole truth, and nothing but the truth?

MARIE/CLARA PEUTHERT. Do you?

(She retrieves a bottle of cheap whisky.)

BETTY/BAILIFF. *(Checking her script.)* You're not supposed to say that!

MARIE/CLARA PEUTHERT. Well, do you?

BETTY/BAILIFF. Yeah.

MARIE/CLARA PEUTHERT. Then so do I. If it's good enough for the Bailiff, it's good enough for Clara Peuthert.

(BETTY returns to her stool.)

DIANE/PROSECUTING ATTORNEY. Clara, can you tell the court where you first met Anastasia?

MARIE/CLARA PEUTHERT. Can you?

DIANE/PROSECUTING ATTORNEY. Where did you first meet the plaintiff?

MARIE/CLARA PEUTHERT. I want to take the fifth! Oh.... Here it is!

(She picks up the bottle of whiskey and drinks.)

DIANE/PROSECUTING ATTORNEY. Clara, are you sober?

ATHENA/DEFENSE ATTORNEY. *(Rising.)* Objection! Irrelevant.

DIANE/PROSECUTING ATTORNEY. Irrelevant? The defendant is so drunk she can't answer the questions!

ATHENA/DEFENSE ATTORNEY. Objection. Just because the defendant does not answer the questions to your liking, doesn't mean that her judgment is impaired.

DIANE/PROSECUTING ATTORNEY. Very well. I withdraw the question. *(ATHENA sits.)* Clara, are you a practicing alcoholic?

ATHENA/DEFENSE ATTORNEY. *(Rising.)* Objection! Irrelevant! My client is not on trial for her personal habits. Counsel is trying to prejudice the jury.

DIANE/PROSECUTING ATTORNEY. The question is whether or not the defendant willfully denied my client her identity. I intend to prove that a practicing alcoholic cannot help but deny another woman her identity, because she is already invested in denying her own.

ATHENA/DEFENSE ATTORNEY. Pure speculation! I object to the fact that Counsel is singling out alcohol abuse as a factor in altering a woman's identity. There are a thousand factors that influence our identities and attempting to isolate any one of them as a determining factor is amateur psychology at its worst. My client's identity, just like the identity of the plaintiff, is a complex and constantly changing set of conditions, not a material entity. Counsel talks as if a woman's identity is like a driver's license—something that is permanently assigned and subject to loss or theft....

DIANE/PROSECUTING ATTORNEY. I am willing to produce expert witnesses who will testify that alcoholism produces a specific set of behaviors and attitudes—

ATHENA/DEFENSE ATTORNEY. We are not here to put the effects of drinking on trial. And if we are, then I submit that one third of our jury should be up here with the defendants.

BETTY/BAILIFF. *(Rising.)* Okay, okay. Well, does Diane get to ask Clara about her drinking habits? What's it going to be? *(She takes the vote.)* Overruled [or Sustained; if Sustained, skip to *].

(BETTY and ATHENA return to their seats.)

DIANE/PROSECUTING ATTORNEY. Clara, are you a practicing alcoholic?

MARIE/CLARA PEUTHERT. No. I think I've got it down by now.

(She laughs.)

DIANE/PROSECUTING ATTORNEY. * And you met my client at Dalldorf Mental Institution, didn't you?

MARIE/CLARA PEUTHERT. Yes.

DIANE/PROSECUTING ATTORNEY. You were a patient on her ward, weren't you?

MARIE/CLARA PEUTHERT. Why are you asking me? You seem to know all the answers.

DIANE/PROSECUTING ATTORNEY. Please answer the question. You were a patient, weren't you?

MARIE/CLARA PEUTHERT. Yes.

DIANE/PROSECUTING ATTORNEY. And what were you committed for?

MARIE/CLARA PEUTHERT. Why don't you ask Thea? Or is that a diagnosis?

DIANE/PROSECUTING ATTORNEY. Why were you at Dalldorf?

MARIE/CLARA PEUTHERT. Because my neighbors thought I stole some money from them.

DIANE/PROSECUTING ATTORNEY. Why did they send you to a mental institution?

MARIE/CLARA PEUTHERT. Born lucky, I guess.

DIANE/PROSECUTING ATTORNEY. Was it because of alcoholism?

MARIE/CLARA PEUTHERT. Ask Thea's boyfriend.

DIANE/PROSECUTING ATTORNEY. And how did you recognize Anastasia?

MARIE/CLARA PEUTHERT. That was easy. Anybody with half a brain—no offense, Thea—could see that she was not your ordinary fruitcake.

DIANE/PROSECUTING ATTORNEY. What do you mean?

MARIE/CLARA PEUTHERT. Anastasia never socialized with the other inmates. She wouldn't go outside either, unless the nurses made sure that everyone else had come in. And she had this way of moving her head, like she was giving you permission to speak, or like she was dismissing you. Anyone who had ever spent time around members of the royal family would have recognized that immediately, but then the nurses wouldn't know anything about that.

DIANE/PROSECUTING ATTORNEY. And when did you have the opportunity to study the members of the upper class?

MARIE/CLARA PEUTHERT. *(With extreme dignity.)* I was a governess in Moscow.

DIANE/PROSECUTING ATTORNEY. I understood you were a laundress.

MARIE/CLARA PEUTHERT. I don't give a shit what you understood! Do you "understand" that?

DIANE/PROSECUTING ATTORNEY. I must warn you about contempt ....

MARIE/CLARA PEUTHERT. Yeah, well you get to call me a washerwoman and a liar, and then I get threatened with a jail sentence when I tell you where to get off, and you want to call it contempt! Just who's denying whose identity here?

DIANE/PROSECUTING ATTORNEY. I'll ask the questions.

MARIE/CLARA PEUTHERT. Right. You just do that, and I'll try to remember my place.

DIANE/PROSECUTING ATTORNEY. Do you *remember* when you first realized who my client was?

MARIE/CLARA PEUTHERT. It must have been either during one of my blackouts or on one of my laundry days....

DIANE/PROSECUTING ATTORNEY. So you *don't* remember?

MARIE/CLARA PEUTHERT. *(Angry at being patronized.)* I remember I knew she was different my first day on the ward, and I remember by the end of my first week that I knew there were only two sane women at Dalldorf—me and her—and that's including those nurses who walked around all day with thermometers up their butts and bedpan breath from kissing doctors' asses. And I remember that I told her she looked like somebody I'd seen before and that she didn't exactly seem to come from the streets, if you know what I mean.

DIANE/PROSECUTING ATTORNEY. And so you—

MARIE/CLARA PEUTHERT. *(Raising her voice to override DIANE.) And* I remember the article in the *Berliner Illustreirte Zeitung* with the cover story titled "The Truth about the Murder of the Tsar," and I remember it said there was a rumor that one of the Tsar's daughters was still alive. And I remember that was when I put two and two together and told her I knew who she was, and I remember she started to cry and pulled the blanket over her face.

DIANE/PROSECUTING ATTORNEY. Did she—

MARIE/CLARA PEUTHERT. *(Rolling right on.) And* I remember after that she started getting friendly with me, and she told me that she had an aunt in Germany she wanted me to write to. And I remember that nobody else in the whole goddamn nut house was willing to lift a finger to help her except for Clara Peuthert—

DIANE/PROSECUTING ATTORNEY. Okay ....

MARIE/CLARA PEUTHERT. *(Louder.)* ... good old kind-hearted Clara Peuthert—

DIANE/PROSECUTING ATTORNEY. All right ....

MARIE/CLARA PEUTHERT. *(Louder still.)* Clara Peuthert who's on trial today, because she was just patsy enough to spring the

Grand Duchess of Russia from the state loony bin!

DIANE/PROSECUTING ATTORNEY. Thank you, Clara.

MARIE/CLARA PEUTHERT. You're welcome, Diane.

DIANE/PROSECUTING ATTORNEY. Did you write to Anastasia's aunt?

MARIE/CLARA PEUTHERT. Shit, yeah, I wrote to the old bitch. Why isn't she here, today? Anastasia's own aunt! *(She stands up and addresses the audience.)* Where is the great Princess Irene of Prussia? How come she isn't here, sitting in the Rogues' Gallery with the rest of us hardened criminals?

DIANE/PROSECUTING ATTORNEY. *(Crossing toward MARIE.)* I think—

MARIE/CLARA PEUTHERT. *(To DIANE.)* Good! That's going to come in handy. *(To audience.)* You know what old Princess Irene did? She showed up for dinner one night, introduced herself under a phony name and pretended not to know her own dead sister's daughter! How's that for humane? How's that for denying identity? You want to know who denied your client's identity?—It wasn't Clara Peuthert! *(Crossing behind the other defendants.)* It was Princess Irene of Prussia and her bitch of a roommate sitting right here!

(She taps AMY's head, messing up her hair.)

AMY/SOPHIE BUXHOEVEDEN. *(To ATHENA.)* I object!

MARIE/CLARA PEUTHERT. *(To AMY.)* Forgive me ... *"Baroness"* Bitch.

DIANE/PROSECUTING ATTORNEY. All right, Clara, you made your point. *(DIANE waits while MARIE, with immense dignity, returns to the witness chair.)* You were released from the mental institution, weren't you?

MARIE/CLARA PEUTHERT. You haven't answered my question. Where is Irene? Didn't she get one of your little subpoenas?

DIANE/PROSECUTING ATTORNEY. No.

MARIE/CLARA PEUTHERT. Why not?

DIANE/PROSECUTING ATTORNEY. I'll ask the questions, if you don't mind—

MARIE/CLARA PEUTHERT. But I do. Where's Irene?

DIANE/PROSECUTING ATTORNEY. What did you do after you were released from Dalldorf?

MARIE/CLARA PEUTHERT. I don't remember. Where's Irene?

DIANE/PROSECUTING ATTORNEY. You contacted some of the members of the Russian aristocracy who had been exiled, didn't you?

MARIE/CLARA PEUTHERT. I don't remember. Where's Irene?

DIANE/PROSECUTING ATTORNEY. And you brought one of them to Dalldorf to see Anastasia, didn't you?

MARIE/CLARA PEUTHERT. I don't remember. Where's Irene?

DIANE/PROSECUTING ATTORNEY. *(After a pause.)* We didn't subpoena Princess Irene because Anastasia didn't want to.

MARIE/CLARA PEUTHERT. *(Rising and crossing down to the audience.)* This is too much! If you're family, you get to do whatever the hell you want to, but if you're just some poor woman in a state institution trying to do a fellow inmate a favor—well, throw the goddamn book at her! *(To BETTY.)* Take a vote on that one, why don't you? *(To audience.)* Or do you all have some little Princess Irene tucked away somewhere? How many of you have some nasty little sadist hiding in the family closet—some mother, or some sister, or some aunt you just can't bear to put on the hot seat, because their testimony might just prove they didn't love you? Well, let me just tell you something—For every Princess Irene you're protecting, there's always going to be some poor innocent Clara Peuthert who's going to get it in the neck for crimes she didn't commit, and you remember that!

(She takes her time returning to the witness chair.)

DIANE/PROSECUTING ATTORNEY. After Anastasia was

released from Dalldorf, she moved in with you, didn't she?

MARIE/CLARA PEUTHERT. And a damned good thing. No one else would take her.

DIANE/PROSECUTING ATTORNEY. And you beat her, didn't you?

ATHENA/DEFENSE ATTORNEY. *(Rising.)* Objection! The defendant is not on trial for assault.

DIANE/PROSECUTING ATTORNEY. *(Outraged.)* The defendant is on trial for denying my client her identity, and the physical violation of a woman is a complete invalidation of her identity.

ATHENA/DEFENSE ATTORNEY. Speculation. My colleague is attempting to characterize every aspect of the defendant's lifestyle and personal habits as criminal acts—

DIANE/PROSECUTING ATTORNEY. Beating a woman is not a lifestyle or personal habit!

BETTY/BAILIFF. *(Rising.)* Okay. Can Diane question Clara about hitting the Grand Duchess? What's it going to be? *(She takes the vote.)* Overruled [or Sustained; if Sustained, skip to *].

(ATHENA and BETTY return to their seats.)

DIANE/PROSECUTING ATTORNEY. You beat the plaintiff during the period she was living with you, didn't you?

MARIE/CLARA PEUTHERT. I might have tried to slap some sense in her.

DIANE/PROSECUTING ATTORNEY. And how many times did you assault Anastasia?

MARIE/CLARA PEUTHERT. I didn't "assault" her. I slapped her a couple of times. I don't remember when.

DIANE/PROSECUTING ATTORNEY. Might it have been when you realized that the royal family was not going to recognize her and that your fellow inmate might turn out to be a financial liability instead of the goose that laid the golden egg?

ATHENA/DEFENSE ATTORNEY. *(Rising.)* Objection! Leading the witness.

DIANE/PROSECUTING ATTORNEY. Very well. Why did you assault Anastasia?

(ATHENA sits.)

MARIE/CLARA PEUTHERT. I didn't assault her. I tried to slap some sense into her.

DIANE/PROSECUTING ATTORNEY. I see. * You threw Anastasia out of your apartment, didn't you?

MARIE/CLARA PEUTHERT. Look, I don't run a hotel. The Grand Duchess wasn't paying any rent—and she wasn't doing any of the work, either. Picture it: Here she is, the richest goddamn woman in Europe, with ten million rubles rotting in some goddamn account in the Bank of England, and all she has to do is get the right people to say she's Anastasia. But does she cooperate? Who's out pounding the pavement? Clara Peuthert! Who's out tracking down all the Russian imperial muck-a-mucks? Clara Peuthert! Who's out talking them into paying us a little visit? Clara Peuthert! And if you think it's easy for a woman who looks like me to walk up to some grand duke and convince him I'm best friends with the Tsar of Russia's daughter, who I happened to meet in the lunatic asylum—well, think again. But I did it. I got them to come see her. And you know what happened? You know how the Grand Duchess of Russia received her visitors? Like that! With a goddamn blanket over her head! And you know what else she did? She wouldn't speak any Russian. I'm trying to prove she's the Tsar of Russia's daughter, and she won't say a word of Russian. German, French, English, yeah. But Russian?—Nyet! And she knows how to speak it all right. You should hear her in her sleep. She talks all night! So how hard can it be to just show a little courtesy, a little smile, a little *"spasiba"* when someone brings you a present? How hard is it to take a goddamn blanket off your head and let them look at you? Is that so goddamn much for me to ask when I've been slaving my whole goddamn life away, working fourteen-hour days, killing myself with work for goddamn near forty years! Is that really so goddamn much to ask? Hell, yeah, I threw her ass out. And I'd throw it out again!

DIANE/PROSECUTING ATTORNEY. Thank you. *(To ATHENA.)* Your witness.

(DIANE sits.)

ATHENA/DEFENSE ATTORNEY. *(She approaches the witness and smiles at her.)* Hi, Clara. I'm just going to ask you a few questions. You've been up here quite a while.

MARIE/CLARA PEUTHERT. *(Directing her comment at DIANE.)* I'm not getting paid for it, either.

ATHENA/DEFENSE ATTORNEY. Clara, can you tell us something about your childhood?

DIANE/PROSECUTING ATTORNEY. *(Rising.)* Objection! Irrelevant!

ATHENA/DEFENSE ATTORNEY. The prosecution is attempting to establish some absolute standard for judging interactions between women. I intend to demonstrate that a woman's ethics are the result of her upbringing.

DIANE/PROSECUTING ATTORNEY. Counsel has gotten off the subject. I object to the introduction of testimony about the defendant's childhood. The conditioning a child receives does not exempt her from taking responsibility for her actions as an adult.

BETTY/BAILIFF. *(Rising.)* Okay, there it is. Athena wants to ask Clara about her childhood. Diane doesn't think it's relevant. Can Athena ask her about her childhood? What's it going to be? *(BETTY takes the vote.)* Overruled [or Sustained; if Sustained, skip to *].

(BETTY and DIANE return to their seats.)

ATHENA/DEFENSE ATTORNEY. Clara, what was your childhood like?

MARIE/CLARA PEUTHERT. I wasn't the Tsar's daughter.

ATHENA/DEFENSE ATTORNEY. Your father was—

MARIE/CLARA PEUTHERT. He was a son-of-a-bitch, and then he was gone. And my mother was a "practicing alcoholic," as they say. And I had six brothers and four sisters, and we all had to work as soon as we could stand. And I've never seen a time since, when I didn't have to work.

ATHENA/DEFENSE ATTORNEY. So you were poor.

MARIE/CLARA PEUTHERT. Yeah, I was poor. *(To JENNY.)* And I'm not talking about being so poor that when you run out of rubles you have to sell your pearls! *(To ATHENA.)* That's what she had to do, you know, when they were smuggling her out of Russia in the back of that cart. She had a string of pearls sewn in the seam of her petticoat—her birthday pearls! Every year on her birthday, they'd give her another one. And she had to sell them! Boo hoo! *(To JENNY.)* You know what kind of "pearls" I had to sell when I ran out of money? And you don't see me crying about it, do you? You don't see me walking around with a coat over my head. *(To ATHENA.)* Her and her pride. I can tell you about pride. I could write a goddamn book about it. You know what I'm proud of? I'm proud of being alive. But you know what? Her—the Imperial Grand Duchess of Russia— she's ashamed because she's not dead!

ATHENA/DEFENSE ATTORNEY. * You tried to help Anastasia, didn't you?

MARIE/CLARA PEUTHERT. Hell, yeah. And a lot of thanks I got for it, too. You know, she had more in one day than most of us ever get in a whole lifetime. She had sixteen goddamn years of luxury, that's what she had—a couple of hard years after that, yeah, sure, so what? If she'd just let go of it and gotten on with her life, you know she could have had it all again.

ATHENA/DEFENSE ATTORNEY. And that's what you were

trying to get her to see?

MARIE/CLARA PEUTHERT. Yeah. You've gotta be tough to survive.

ATHENA/DEFENSE ATTORNEY. So that's what you were doing?—toughening Anastasia up?

DIANE/PROSECUTING ATTORNEY. *(Rising.)* Objection. The witness' motives are irrelevant. We are concerned with her actions.

ATHENA/DEFENSE ATTORNEY. It is impossible to judge my client's actions without understanding her motives.

BETTY/BAILIFF. *(Rising.)* So…. Does Athena get to ask why Clara treated Anastasia the way she did? What's it going to be? *(She takes the vote.)* Overruled [or Sustained; if Sustained, skip to *].

(BETTY and DIANE return to their seats.)

ATHENA/DEFENSE ATTORNEY. So you saw your behaviors toward Anastasia as being protective, didn't you?

MARIE/CLARA PEUTHERT. Yeah. Look at the girl! How the hell do you think she was going to make it on the street?

ATHENA/DEFENSE ATTORNEY. * It was Anastasia's idea to come live with you after she left Dalldorf, wasn't it?

MARIE/CLARA PEUTHERT. Yes. I was her friend.

ATHENA/DEFENSE ATTORNEY. Thank you.

DIANE/PROSECUTING ATTORNEY. *(Rising.)* I just have one more question to ask you.

MARIE/CLARA PEUTHERT. I can't wait.

DIANE/PROSECUTING ATTORNEY. Did it ever occur to you that the woman you were "slapping some sense into" might not have been a spoiled brat, but a severely traumatized and emotionally disturbed human being?

MARIE/CLARA PEUTHERT. Hell, that woman—*(She points to JENNY.)* She's no crazier than I am.

DIANE/PROSECUTING ATTORNEY. *(Smiling.)* No further

questions. *(To BETTY.)* Please call the next witness.

(DIANE sits.)

BETTY/BAILIFF. *(Rising.)* Baroness Sophie Karlovna Buxhoeveden to the stand, please.

(MARIE passes AMY on the way to the stand, and swats her with one of her shopping bags.)

MARIE. Stinking little traitor!
AMY. *(Grabbing the handle of the bag.)* You hit me!
MARIE. Let go!
AMY. No! *You* hit me!

(The two women begin wrestling and shouting over the bag.)

DIANE/PROSECUTING ATTORNEY. *(Rising.)* Bailiff!
BETTY. *(Checking.)* This isn't in the script! She's not supposed to do that! *(Crossing to MARIE and AMY, BETTY tries to separate them.)* What's the idea? This isn't in the script!
MARIE. Neither is leaving before the second act, is it "Baroness?"
AMY. I don't know what you're talking about.
MARIE. Let me refresh your memory. The nightclub act at the Eastland Hotel tonight?
AMY. *(Lunging toward MELISSA.)* You little snitch.
MELISSA. I didn't say anything!
AMY. *(To MARIE.)* Did she tell you she was going to trade roles with me? Did she tell you that?
MELISSA. That's not true!
AMY. Oh, yeah?
ATHENA. I move to place Sophie Buxhoeveden under arrest for

contempt of court.

AMY. *(Indicating MARIE.)* She's the one who attacked me!

MARIE. *(To AMY.)* You're the one walking out on the company! Athena heard you tell Melissa!

LISA. *(Appearing from the wings.)* What's going on? This isn't in my play!

ATHENA. *(Indicating AMY.)* Bailiff, arrest that woman!

MARIE. Oh, shove it up your ass, Athena. You're no better than she is. You were supposed to play Anastasia tonight. What about that?

ATHENA. *(Indicating MARIE.)* I move to place Clara Peuthert under arrest for assault and battery.

MARIE. Screw you, Athena!

ATHENA. And contempt of court.

BETTY/BAILIFF. *(To ATHENA.)* But it's not in the script!

DONNA. *(To ATHENA.)* It's not Marie's fault!

LISA. *(Pointing to MARIE.)* She's out of character!

DONNA. Athena is the one who's trying to steal the show!

ATHENA. Bailiff, you will please remove Fraulein Peuthert and Baroness Buxhoeveden.

MARIE. *(Backing away from BETTY.)* Lay a hand on me, Betty, and so help me—

BETTY. I'm an actor, now! You can't talk to me like that!

DIANE. *(Stepping quickly between BETTY and MARIE.)* If it please the court, I move that we adjourn for a brief recess.

AMY. No! What about my scene? I have to play my scene!

MARIE. *(Pushing AMY.)* Don't worry, you'll have plenty of time—in the second act!

AMY. *(Pushing back.)* I won't play it at all!

MARIE. *(Pushing her again.)* I don't think you have that choice.

DIANE. *(To BETTY.)* Call for the motion!

LISA. But it's not the end of the act!

(MARIE shoves AMY. The actors are on the verge of violence.)

DIANE. *(To BETTY.)* The motion! Call for it!

BETTY/BAILIFF. *(Crossing to the audience, while the actors argue with AMY.)* Quick! Green cards for a recess! Hold them up! *(A triumph for the people.)* That does it! This court is now adjourned for a ten-minute recess.

(At the word adjourned, AMY tries to exit up right, but she is mobbed by a company of angry, shouting actors.)

DIANE. *(Crossing down front and shouting toward the light booth.)* Blackout! Blackout!

(All hell breaks lose. Blackout.)

END OF ACT I

ACT II

(Lights come up on the courtroom setting for the Emma Goldman Theater Brigade production. Curtain rises as the actors file in and take their seats in grim silence: MELISSA crosses to the downstage defendant's chair. She is followed by DIANE, who escorts JENNY, under the coat, to the plaintiff's chair. MARIE and DONNA enter with AMY between them. They are holding her arms as they escort her to the defendants' chairs. Finally BETTY enters, giggling uncontrollably as she crosses to her stool. DIANE glares at her.)

BETTY/BAILIFF. *(Rising, struggling to keep a straight face.)* The Women's Court is now in session. The Court calls Baroness Sophie Karlovna Buxhoeveden to the stand. *(BETTY crosses to the witness chair. Throwing off MARIE and DONNA, AMY rises and crosses to the witness chair. During her testimony, she will avoid looking at JENNY.)* State your name please.

AMY/SOPHIE BUXHOEVEDEN. Baroness Sophie Buxhoeveden.
BETTY/BAILIFF. Do you swear to tell the truth, the whole truth, and nothing but the truth?
MARIE/CLARA PEUTHERT. That'll be the day!
AMY/SOPHIE BUXHOEVEDEN. I do.

(BETTY crosses back to her stool.)

59

DIANE/PROSECUTING ATTORNEY. *(Rising.)* Could you state your relationship to the plaintiff, please?

MARIE/CLARA PEUTHERT. Executioner.

DIANE/PROSECUTING ATTORNEY. *(To ATHENA.)* Counselor, please! *(ATHENA speaks to MARIE privately.)* Your relationship to the plaintiff?

AMY/SOPHIE BUXHOEVEDEN. I was the maid of honor to the Empress Alexandra—

DIANE/PROSECUTING ATTORNEY. Anastasia's mother—

AMY/SOPHIE BUXHOEVEDEN. Yes, the maid of honor to the Empress and a member of the imperial suite for five years.

DIANE/PROSECUTING ATTORNEY. So you lived with the royal family, didn't you?

AMY/SOPHIE BUXHOEVEDEN. I lived with them until the family was sent into exile.

DIANE/PROSECUTING ATTORNEY. You didn't live with them in prison?

AMY/SOPHIE BUXHOEVEDEN. No.

DIANE/PROSECUTING ATTORNEY. But you were sent to Siberia also?

AMY/SOPHIE BUXHOEVEDEN. I was sent to Siberia in 1917 at the same time the royal family was exiled, but I did not live with them.

DIANE/PROSECUTING ATTORNEY. And why not?

AMY/SOPHIE BUXHOEVEDEN. The Bolsheviks would not allow it.

DIANE/PROSECUTING ATTORNEY. But when they moved the family a second time, to the prison at Ekaterinburg—

(JENNY reacts violently to the name.)

AMY/SOPHIE BUXHOEVEDEN. No, I did not live with them there either. I escorted the children on the train to Ekaterinburg—

(JENNY reacts again.)

DIANE/PROSECUTING ATTORNEY. You were chosen to escort the children to the place where they would die?

AMY/SOPHIE BUXHOEVEDEN. I did not know that at the time. We were not even told where the train was going. I was told they would be joining their parents, that was all. *(She reflects.)* I tried to make it a happy trip for them.

DIANE/PROSECUTING ATTORNEY. But you didn't stay with them?

AMY/SOPHIE BUXHOEVEDEN. When we arrived at Ek—at the town, the children were taken away. I did not see them again.

DIANE/PROSECUTING ATTORNEY. I understand that the family doctor, the cook, the valet and a serving girl were allowed to join them in the prison. Why do you suppose the maid of honor was not allowed to serve her Empress in her last days?

MARIE/CLARA PEUTHERT. *(Rising.)* Yeah!

ATHENA/DEFENSE ATTORNEY. *(Rising.)* Objection! Counsel is asking the witness to speculate.

DIANE/PROSECUTING ATTORNEY. Not at all. I thought perhaps Baroness Buxhoeveden might know the reason why she was treated so differently from the other members of the imperial suite.

(ATHENA sits.)

AMY/SOPHIE BUXHOEVEDEN. I have no idea. Who knows how a Bolshevik thinks?

MARIE/CLARA PEUTHERT. Another Bolshevik!

DIANE/PROSECUTING ATTORNEY. And so they shot, stabbed, and bludgeoned the entire family to death—along with the physician, the cook, the valet and the serving girl, but they let the maid of honor go free. In fact, they allowed her to leave the country. Is that right?

AMY/SOPHIE BUXHOEVEDEN. I left the country, yes.

DIANE/PROSECUTING ATTORNEY. And yet, you were a Baroness, were you not? A member of the hated aristocracy?

AMY/SOPHIE BUXHOEVEDEN. Yes.

DIANE/PROSECUTING ATTORNEY. Why did they let you leave the country when they killed everyone else?

ATHENA/DEFENSE ATTORNEY. *(Rising.)* Objection! Counsel is asking the witness to speculate.

DIANE/PROSECUTING ATTORNEY. *(Ignoring ATHENA.)* Could it have been because you had done them a favor?

MARIE/CLARA PEUTHERT. Yes!

ATHENA/DEFENSE ATTORNEY. Objection!

DIANE/PROSECUTING ATTORNEY. Could it have been that you shared certain information—

MARIE/CLARA PEUTHERT. Yes!

ATHENA/DEFENSE ATTORNEY. Objection! This entire line of questioning is based on hearsay and speculation. The question at hand is Baroness Buxhoeveden's failure to identify the plaintiff during her stay at Dalldorf Mental Asylum. These questions are irrelevant and prejudicial.

DIANE/PROSECUTING ATTORNEY. Very well, then. Let's talk about that visit to Dalldorf.

(ATHENA sits.)

MARIE/CLARA PEUTHERT. Talk about that visit, Baroness! Talk about how you murdered that girl twice, you ....

DIANE/PROSECUTING ATTORNEY. *(To ATHENA.)* Counsel, please! *(ATHENA pulls MARIE back to her chair.)* When did this visit occur?

AMY/SOPHIE BUXHOEVEDEN. March 12, 1922.

DIANE/PROSECUTING ATTORNEY. That would have been four years after the supposed murder of the imperial family, wouldn't it?

AMY/SOPHIE BUXHOEVEDEN. Yes.

DIANE/PROSECUTING ATTORNEY. And you were living in Germany, weren't you?

MARIE/CLARA PEUTHERT. She was living with that bitch Princess Irene. They were in on it together!

AMY/SOPHIE BUXHOEVEDEN. *(To DIANE.)* Do you want me to answer the questions?

DIANE/PROSECUTING ATTORNEY. Please. Can you tell us about this visit to Dalldorf?

AMY/SOPHIE BUXHOEVEDEN. This woman, Clara Peuthert, had been stirring up a lot of rumors in the community of emigrants—

MARIE/CLARA PEUTHERT. Rumors, my ass!

AMY/SOPHIE BUXHOEVEDEN. *(To DIANE.)* Do you want me to continue?

DIANE/PROSECUTING ATTORNEY. Please.

AMY/SOPHIE BUXHOEVEDEN. And I was asked to go to Dalldorf and visit the invalid to identify her. You see, I had been the last member of the imperial suite to see the family before they disappeared.

MARIE/CLARA PEUTHERT. *(She rises. BETTY crosses to restrain her, but MARIE circles behind the defendants.)* Disappeared, my ass! Before they were shot, Baroness! Shot in a pile in a courtyard, hacked to pieces, and incinerated! *(BETTY grabs her and escorts her back to her chair.)* Get your hands off me! You want the truth? I'm telling it! I'm telling the truth, because you won't get it from Baroness Bolshevik over there.

DIANE/PROSECUTING ATTORNEY. *(To MARIE.)* Clara, if the witness is lying, please grant that we have enough intelligence to figure that out for ourselves. *(MARIE sits down, and BETTY returns to her stool.)* And so you went to Dalldorf to identify Anastasia?

AMY/SOPHIE BUXHOEVEDEN. No. I went to Dalldorf to identify the Grand Duchess Tatiana. I had been told that the invalid was the second oldest daughter, not Anastasia.

MARIE/CLARA PEUTHERT. Bullshit! You knew it was Anastasia!

AMY/SOPHIE BUXHOEVEDEN. I was told that the woman was claiming to be the Grand Duchess Tatiana.

MARIE/CLARA PEUTHERT. And who told you that? An aunt who wanted to get her hands on the family fortune? Who told you that?

AMY/SOPHIE BUXHOEVEDEN. I went to the ward of the hospital, and she was hiding under the blankets—

MARIE/CLARA PEUTHERT. I wonder why! Hiding from a murderer!

AMY/SOPHIE BUXHOEVEDEN. *(Rising in indignation.)* I cannot answer your questions with that woman in the courtroom.

MARIE/CLARA PEUTHERT. Why? Because I know you're lying? *(BETTY crosses to MARIE, and she turns on her.)* Why should I leave?

BETTY/BAILIFF. Because it's in the script—See?

MARIE/CLARA PEUTHERT. *(To BETTY.)* All right. I see it. *(BETTY escorts MARIE out of the courtroom. MARIE exits shouting:)* Who paid you this time, Baroness? Huh? Who paid you this time?

(AMY sits.)

DIANE/PROSECUTING ATTORNEY. *(To AMY.)* So Anastasia was hiding under the blankets?

AMY/SOPHIE BUXHOEVEDEN. Yes. And so we took the blankets off her face and got her to stand up, and I saw immediately that she was too short to be Tatiana, and I said so.

DIANE/PROSECUTING ATTORNEY. And what were your exact words?

AMY/SOPHIE BUXHOEVEDEN. "She's too short for Tatiana."

DIANE/PROSECUTING ATTORNEY. But you didn't notice if

she was too short for Anastasia.

AMY/SOPHIE BUXHOEVEDEN. I went there to see if the girl was Tatiana. She was not, and I said so. It was not my job to determine who else she might have been.

DIANE/PROSECUTING ATTORNEY. And so you left.

AMY/SOPHIE BUXHOEVEDEN. Yes.

DIANE/PROSECUTING ATTORNEY. Immediately.

AMY/SOPHIE BUXHOEVEDEN. Yes.

DIANE/PROSECUTING ATTORNEY. And you never went back for a second visit?

AMY/SOPHIE BUXHOEVEDEN. It was not necessary. She was too short to be Tatiana.

DIANE/PROSECUTING ATTORNEY. Thank you. *(To ATHENA.)* Your witness.

(DIANE crosses to her chair and sits.)

ATHENA/DEFENSE ATTORNEY. *(Rising.)* Baroness, when you rode with the children to Ekaterinburg—*(JENNY reacts.)* did you ask how they had been treated?

AMY/SOPHIE BUXHOEVEDEN. It was not something they wanted to talk about. We spoke about happier times, about the scenery.

ATHENA/DEFENSE ATTORNEY. The girls would have been seventeen, nineteen, twenty-one, and twenty-three—would they not?

AMY/SOPHIE BUXHOEVEDEN. *(A long pause. ATHENA turns to face her client.)* Yes.

ATHENA/DEFENSE ATTORNEY. And they had been left with the members of the Red Army—the Bolsheviks.

AMY/SOPHIE BUXHOEVEDEN. *(A longer pause.)* Yes.

ATHENA/DEFENSE ATTORNEY. The girls were not allowed to lock their bedroom doors at night. Do you know why?

AMY/SOPHIE BUXHOEVEDEN. *(Another pause.)* Who understands the mind of a Bolshevik?

ATHENA/DEFENSE ATTORNEY. *(Crossing slowly behind AMY.)* Did you notice any change in the girls from when you had last seen them?

AMY/SOPHIE BUXHOEVEDEN. *(Losing her composure.)* Yes, of course. This is stupid. Yes, of course they were changed. They had been prisoners for a year! I know what you want me to say. They had been raped, hadn't they? Yes, of course, they had been raped. Many times. They were scared. They were afraid they were going to die. *(To the audience.)* We were all afraid we were going to die. What was the use of talking about it? It was a war, it was a nightmare. What do you want me to say? Do you want me to pull a blanket over my head, too? Is that going to make you all feel sorry for me? It was a war. Do you understand? We were all prisoners. We did what we were told. Some of us survived. Some of us didn't.

ATHENA/DEFENSE ATTORNEY. You don't like to think about this period of your life do you?

AMY/SOPHIE BUXHOEVEDEN. No. What would be the point? There! *(Finally turning in the direction of JENNY, she points to her, concentrating her fury on the victim.)* There is someone who thinks about it!

ATHENA/DEFENSE ATTORNEY. Thank you, Baroness.

(She sits. AMY returns to her defendant's chair.)

DIANE/PROSECUTING ATTORNEY. *(Reading from the rewrites.)* Please call Baroness Zinaida Tolstoy.

(Looking up, she realizes that BETTY is off stage. There is a long pause.)

BETTY. *(Offstage.)* Shit!

(The loud sounds of objects falling and possibly breaking. BETTY

races onstage, stops abruptly, and then strolls calmly to her stool.)

DIANE/PROSECUTING ATTORNEY. Please call Baroness Zinaida Tolstoy.

BETTY/BAILIFF. *(Consulting her script.)* But it says "Shura Tegleva."

DIANE. *(Whispering.)* This is the new character. It's part of the rewrites. Here, check your sheets.

BETTY/BAILIFF. *(Looking at the pages ATHENA gave her in Act I.)* Oh, right. Baroness Zinaida Tolstoy to the stand. *(LISA enters wearing a Russian scarf. She carries a copy of the rewrites. All of the actors read from these pages during all of ZINAIDA's testimony. BETTY crosses to swear her in.)* State your name, please.

LISA/ZINAIDA TOLSTOY. Zinaida Sergeievna Tolstoy.

BETTY/BAILIFF. Do you swear to tell the truth, the whole truth, and nothing but the truth?

LISA/ZINAIDA TOLSTOY. I do.

(BETTY returns to her stool.)

DIANE/PROSECUTING ATTORNEY. *(Rising.)* Baroness, what is your relationship to the plaintiff?

LISA ZINAIDA TOLSTOY. I was a close friend of her mother's. And after Anastasia was released from the mental asylum—before she went to Clara's—I nursed her.

DIANE/PROSECUTING ATTORNEY. Anastasia was ill?

LISA/ZINAIDA TOLSTOY. Yes. She had a fever from the bayonet wound in her arm. It was tubercular, you know. The doctors had to give her morphine.

DIANE/PROSECUTING ATTORNEY. So, Anastasia was drugged with narcotics?

LISA/ZINAIDA TOLSTOY. Yes.

(ATHENA, DIANE, LISA and BETTY turn the pages of the rewrites simultaneously.)

DIANE/PROSECUTING ATTORNEY. And you say you nursed her during this period?

LISA/ZINAIDA TOLSTOY. Yes. I moved into the sickroom with her.

DIANE/PROSECUTING ATTORNEY. Can you tell the court how the morphine affected the Grand Duchess?

LISA/ZINAIDA TOLSTOY. She was dazed, and she would speak in Russian, a language she wouldn't remember when she was conscious.

DIANE/PROSECUTING ATTORNEY. So she would speak to you?

LISA/ZINAIDA TOLSTOY. Oh, yes. She would answer my questions. And always in Russian.

DIANE/PROSECUTING ATTORNEY. What did she talk about?

LISA/ZINAIDA TOLSTOY. She told the story.

DIANE/PROSECUTING ATTORNEY. And what story is that?

LISA/ZINAIDA TOLSTOY. About the massacre and the escape.

DIANE/PROSECUTING ATTORNEY. And is it true that prior to the use of morphine, Anastasia would not discuss these experiences—would not even acknowledge that she knew Russian?

LISA/ZINAIDA TOLSTOY. Yes, that's true.

DIANE/PROSECUTING ATTORNEY. Was it your impression then that the morphine allowed Anastasia to access parts of her memory which, because of the trauma, were not available to her conscious mind?

ATHENA/DEFENSE ATTORNEY. *(Rising.)* Objection. Asking the witness to speculate.

DIANE/PROSECUTING ATTORNEY. Withdrawn. *(ATHENA, DIANE, LISA and BETTY turn the pages of the rewrites simultaneously.)* Baroness, did you believe Anastasia?

LISA/ZINAIDA TOLSTOY. Oh, yes.

DIANE/PROSECUTING ATTORNEY. And did she mention Baroness Buxhoeveden?

LISA/ZINAIDA TOLSTOY. Yes. She called her "our Isa."

DIANE/PROSECUTING ATTORNEY. And what did she say about "our Isa?"

ATHENA/DEFENSE ATTORNEY. *(Rising.)* Objection! Hearsay!

DIANE/PROSECUTING ATTORNEY. *(Consulting the rewrites.)* Counselor, that objection is not in my script.

LISA. That's right!

ATHENA/DEFENSE ATTORNEY. Then I know the law better than the playwright. Third-party hearsay is not admissible as evidence.

DIANE/PROSECUTING ATTORNEY. I believe the reason the playwright has written Zinaida into the script is because my client is not capable of testifying on her own behalf—

ATHENA/DEFENSE ATTORNEY. Then maybe she should never have brought suit against my clients.

DIANE/PROSECUTING ATTORNEY. The Women's Court has filed on her behalf—and on behalf of all survivors who cannot plead their own cases.

ATHENA/DEFENSE ATTORNEY. Let's not grandstand, please. The issue here is justice for my clients, and I cannot allow hearsay testimony to be admitted to the record.

DIANE/PROSECUTING ATTORNEY. It's just not your call, Athena. It's in the script.

ATHENA/DEFENSE ATTORNEY. The issue of justice supercedes the social protocol, and the prerogatives of a harried playwright who has no training in law.

DIANE/PROSECUTING ATTORNEY. Then the jury will have to decide.

LISA. No!

ATHENA/DEFENSE ATTORNEY. *(Ignoring the playwright.)*

Let me state my objection plainly, then. *(To the audience.)* Zinaida Tolstoy has been written into this script specifically to report on statements purportedly made by a seriously brain-damaged woman who was under the influence of narcotics at the time when she made these statements. Will the Women's Court allow a woman to be judged and condemned on the strength of what another woman has overheard about her?

DIANE/PROSECUTING ATTORNEY. *(Applauding.)* Bravo, Counselor. It's obvious that my colleague has experience in the men's court, where—for obvious reasons—the emphasis is on the rights of the accused. In the Women's Court, however, we are concerned with the rights of the victims, the survivors, the women who are silenced, censored, invisible, erased. We are concerned with the rights of children, who can't put the events in the right order. We are concerned with the rights of girls, who can't remember anything except their feelings. We are concerned with the rights of the brain-damaged women, the women like my client, whose trauma is so massive, she can only access those files of her memory under heavy sedation or hypnosis. Believe me, nothing would make me happier, or make my job easier, than to put my client on the witness stand. But, women of the jury, the very fact that she is not capable of testifying should be the most compelling argument on her behalf. Zinaida Tolstoy has been privy to the secret files of my client's mind, and I ask, in fairness to my client, that she be allowed to divulge the contents of those files where they have bearing on the guilt—or innocence of the accused.

BETTY/BAILIFF. *(Rising.)* Okay, you've heard ....

ATHENA/DEFENSE ATTORNEY. Excuse me, Bailiff. *(To DIANE.)* Counselor, I need to advise you, if Zinaida Tolstoy testifies, I will call Anastasia to the stand to corroborate.

LISA. You can't do that! It's not part of the play!

DIANE/PROSECUTING ATTORNEY. My client is obviously not capable of testifying.

ATHENA/DEFENSE ATTORNEY. And hearsay is obviously inadmissible.

DIANE/PROSECUTING ATTORNEY. I'll object.

ATHENA/DEFENSE ATTORNEY. Then I will appeal to the jury to override your objection.

DIANE/PROSECUTING ATTORNEY. You're not going to intimidate me, and I won't allow you to intimidate my client. *(To BETTY.)* Bailiff—the ruling on the motion, please.

BETTY/BAILIFF. What was it?

DIANE/PROSECUTING ATTORNEY. If I can question Zinaida about what she heard Anastasia saying—

BETTY/BAILIFF. Oh, yeah. *(To audience.)* Okay.... Can Diane ask Zinaida what she overheard Anastasia saying on morphine? *(She takes the vote.)* Overruled [or Sustained; if Sustained, skip to *].

(ATHENA and BETTY return to their seats.)

DIANE/PROSECUTING ATTORNEY. *(She resumes reading from the rewrites.)* Will you please tell the court what Anastasia told you about Baroness Sophie Buxhoeveden?

LISA/ZINAIDA TOLSTOY. *(Reading again also.)* She told me that while they were prisoners in Ekaterinburg—*(JENNY reacts.)* While they were prisoners, her mother and father talked about how Isa—the Baroness—had changed since the exile. She had become cold and disrespectful. Anastasia told me that her parents believed that Isa betrayed their rescue plans, and that this was why she had changed.

DIANE/PROSECUTING ATTORNEY. Thank you.

(She crosses to her chair and sits.)

ATHENA/DEFENSE ATTORNEY. *(Rising.)* No questions. * I'd like to call Anastasia Romanov to the stand, please.

(LISA, who had begun to step down, returns to the witness chair.)

LISA. No!

DIANE/PROSECUTING ATTORNEY. *(Rising.)* Objection! The Grand Duchess is not medically competent to undergo testifying.

LISA. This is not in the script. You can't do this!

ATHENA/DEFENSE ATTORNEY. *(To DIANE.)* Do you have a doctor's certificate?

DIANE/PROSECUTING ATTORNEY. No. It's obvious from her condition.

ATHENA/DEFENSE ATTORNEY. It's not unheard of for a plaintiff to fake a condition for the benefit of the jury.

DIANE/PROSECUTING ATTORNEY. *(Exasperated.)* I withdraw my objection.

LISA. Diane, what are you doing?

BETTY/BAILIFF. Anastasia Romanov to the stand.

LISA. No! You'll ruin the play!

ATHENA/DEFENSE ATTORNEY. *(To BETTY.)* Please escort the witness to the stand.

(BETTY approaches JENNY and puts her hand on her arm. JENNY reacts violently, with a prolonged scream of an animal being tortured. ATHENA—and, indeed, everyone—is shocked by this sound.)

DIANE/PROSECUTING ATTORNEY. *(Glaring at ATHENA, she instructs BETTY.)* Call the next witness.

BETTY/BAILIFF. Shura Tegleva to the stand, please. *(LISA crosses to the defendants' chairs and sits. DONNA takes the stand, and BETTY crosses to her to swear her in.)* State your name, please.

DONNA/SHURA TEGLEVA. Shura Tegleva.

BETTY/BAILIFF. Do you swear to tell the truth, the whole truth, and nothing but the truth?

DONNA/SHURA TEGLEVA. I do.

(BETTY returns to her stool.)

DIANE/PROSECUTING ATTORNEY. Will you state your relationship to the plaintiff?

DONNA/SHURA TEGLEVA. *(Looking fondly at JENNY.)* I nursed her from the time she was born.

DIANE/PROSECUTING ATTORNEY. And you continued to be her nurse up until the time of the exile, didn't you?

DONNA/SHURA TEGLEVA. Yes.

DIANE/PROSECUTING ATTORNEY. And—

DONNA/SHURA TEGLEVA. *(Cutting her off quickly)* I loved her…. I love her now.

DIANE/PROSECUTING ATTORNEY. Then why was it you failed to recognize her?

DONNA/SHURA TEGLEVA. But that's not true! I did! I came to the hospital when she had the fever. I came and visited her. She asked for me. And I remember the first day—She was lying there, poor thing—so sick. She must not have weighed more than seventy pounds. She was so sick. And I asked them to show me her feet—

DIANE/PROSECUTING ATTORNEY. Can you tell us why you wanted to see her feet?

DONNA/SHURA TEGLEVA. The Grand Duchess' feet were very unusual. The big toe was bent in over the other toes, making a bunion. She was born that way. And the right foot was worse than the left. It was always a problem for us finding shoes—

DIANE/PROSECUTING ATTORNEY. *(Cutting her off.)* And did you identify the feet?

DONNA/SHURA TEGLEVA. Oh, yes. I said right out loud— right there in front of the doctors—"Yes, that's her feet all right. Those are the feet of the Grand Duchess Anastasia Nicolaievna. That's her feet. That's them."

DIANE/PROSECUTING ATTORNEY. And what did you do after that?

DONNA/SHURA TEGLEVA. I came back later when she was awake—she was asleep that first time—and she took this bottle of cologne, the little Schwibsik—

DIANE/PROSECUTING ATTORNEY. Schwibsik?

DONNA/SHURA TEGLEVA. Imp. That was her nickname. She was always full of mischief, so we called her Schwibsik. *(A pause.)* Anyway, she took the bottle of cologne—the one by the bed—and she poured some of it into my hand. She wanted me to put it on her forehead. You see? I laughed so hard the tears ran down my face. They did! The little Schwibsik! She was crazy about perfume. She used to pour it all over her Shura and then tell me she wanted me to be as fragrant as a bouquet. You see? Who else would have known that?

DIANE/PROSECUTING ATTORNEY. And so you say you identified Anastasia?

DONNA/SHURA TEGLEVA. I visited her. We talked. She had a kitten in her hospital room …"Kiki." *(To JENNY.)* Remember Kiki? *(To DIANE.)* She was happy. She would ask for me.

DIANE/PROSECUTING ATTORNEY. But you stopped coming.

DONNA/SHURA TEGLEVA. I lived in Switzerland. I couldn't visit forever, could I?

DIANE/PROSECUTING ATTORNEY. But you stopped writing to her. You wouldn't answer her letters.

DONNA/SHURA TEGLEVA. I'm sorry. I'm not a writer of letters.

DIANE/PROSECUTING ATTORNEY. You stopped coming, you stopped writing. When others began to say she was an imposter, you kept quiet.

DONNA/SHURA TEGLEVA. There were others in a better position to come forward.

DIANE/PROSECUTING ATTORNEY. But you knew who she was and you said nothing.

DONNA/SHURA TEGLEVA. I was never asked.

DIANE/PROSECUTING ATTORNEY. The Grand Duchess asked. I understand that she asked for you repeatedly. "Where is Shura?" "When is Shura coming?" *(DONNA looks down.)* Do you know what she said? She said, "If they had asked Shura to let herself be shot, so that we might live, she would have done it."

DONNA/SHURA TEGLEVA. You don't understand.

DIANE/PROSECUTING ATTORNEY. No, apparently, I don't.

(She sits.)

ATHENA/DEFENSE ATTORNEY. *(Rising.)* Shura, you're married aren't you?

DONNA/SHURA TEGLEVA. *(Scared.)* Yes.

ATHENA/DEFENSE ATTORNEY. And will you tell the court who your husband is?

DIANE/PROSECUTING ATTORNEY. *(Rising.)* Objection! Counsel is now going to claim indemnity for her client, because she's married.

ATHENA/DEFENSE ATTORNEY. My client cut off contact with Anastasia. I have a right to explore whether or not that was in deference to her husband's wishes.

DIANE/PROSECUTING ATTORNEY. Irrelevant! A woman always has the choice to defy her husband!

MELISSA. That's not true!

LISA. You don't have a line here!

MELISSA. I was married to a man who had guns all over the house, and he wouldn't let me talk to my friends, and when they tried to come over—

LISA. *(Cutting her off.)* This is not in my play!

AMY. What play? This isn't a play.

BETTY/BAILIFF. *(Rising.)* Okay, can Athena ask Shura about her husband? *(She takes the vote.)* Overruled [or Sustained; if

Sustained, skip to *].

(BETTY and DIANE return to their seats.)

ATHENA/DEFENSE ATTORNEY. *(To DONNA.)* Who is your husband?

DONNA/SHURA TEGLEVA. Monsieur Pierre Gilliard.

ATHENA/DEFENSE ATTORNEY. He was the tutor for the Tsar's children, wasn't he?

DONNA/SHURA TEGLEVA. Yes.

ATHENA/DEFENSE ATTORNEY. And Mr. Gilliard also came to see Anastasia in the hospital, didn't he?

DONNA/SHURA TEGLEVA. Yes.

ATHENA/DEFENSE ATTORNEY. But his visits were not so happy, were they?

DONNA/SHURA TEGLEVA. *(A pause.)* No.

ATHENA/DEFENSE ATTORNEY. You are under oath. Why were his visits unhappy?

DONNA/SHURA TEGLEVA. *(Very quiet.)* She would not speak to him.

ATHENA/DEFENSE ATTORNEY. And why was that?

DONNA/SHURA TEGLEVA. Because he would ask her about … *(Searching for the correct words.)* the things that happened at the end.

ATHENA/DEFENSE ATTORNEY. And she would not talk about that, would she?

DONNA/SHURA TEGLEVA. No.

ATHENA/DEFENSE ATTORNEY. Why was your husband so rude?

DONNA/SHURA TEGLEVA. *(Alarmed.)* I never said that he was rude.

ATHENA/DEFENSE ATTORNEY. I know. I did. Why do you think he asked her those questions?

DONNA/SHURA TEGLEVA. He ... he had been asked to see her.

ATHENA/DEFENSE ATTORNEY. By whom? *(DONNA says nothing.)* You are under oath.

DONNA/SHURA TEGLEVA. By members of her family.

ATHENA/DEFENSE ATTORNEY. Members who would not come themselves?

DONNA/SHURA TEGLEVA. No.

ATHENA/DEFENSE ATTORNEY. Members who wanted the world to believe she was an imposter?

DONNA/SHURA TEGLEVA. I don't know. Please—

ATHENA/DEFENSE ATTORNEY. Shura, I am *defending* you. *(DONNA sinks back into her chair.)* And so Anastasia was happy to see you, because you played with her kitten and splashed her with cologne, but she was not happy to see your husband?

DONNA/SHURA TEGLEVA. No.

THENA/DEFENSE ATTORNEY. And did this cause problems in your marriage?

DONNA/SHURA TEGLEVA. *(A pause.)* Yes.

ATHENA/DEFENSE ATTORNEY. Your husband published a book shortly after this, didn't he? And it was so popular, he went all over Europe giving lectures on the subject, didn't he? Can you tell us the name of the book?

DONNA/SHURA TEGLEVA. *(With great reluctance.)* The *False Anastasia.*

ATHENA/DEFENSE ATTORNEY. *(To DIANE.)* * Your witness.

(ATHENA sits.)

DIANE/PROSECUTING ATTORNEY. No questions.

ATHENA/DEFENSE ATTORNEY. *(To BETTY.)* I would like to recall Zinaida Tolstoy to the stand

DIANE/PROSECUTING ATTORNEY. This isn't in the script!

ATHENA/DEFENSE ATTORNEY. *(To BETTY.)* Call Zinaida Tolstoy.

DIANE/PROSECUTING ATTORNEY. This is unfair to the rest of us, Athena. When you go off book like this, none of us knows what's going on. You're making yourself look good at our expense.

MARIE. *(Re-entering with her script.)* I just want to point out something—I just want to say that when my character has a few spontaneous remarks—in character, mind you, she gets hauled off the stage, but notice when the daughter of a rich man, who happens to be playing an attorney through some miraculous displacement of collective process—when this rich man's daughter reroutes the entire play, everyone is willing to go along with it! Enough is enough!

MELISSA. *(Inspired by MARIE's impromptu speech, she rises and crosses center stage, ever mindful of the presence of the critics.)* That's right.... Because there's more to art than entertainment. *(Stunned, MARIE sits. During MELISSA's speech, the other actors sit in various frozen attitudes of horror or disbelief.)* That's the whole point of the play. It's not a love story. Women have been Beaverbrooked and Twickendicked to death, riding on buses and subways all over the world while Lady Cecily bats her eyelashes at the factories, and the assembly lines, and the sweatshops, and the drunken, reeling husbands who are waiting at home for their wives to return from the masquerade ball—waiting arrogantly, with the groceries, and the rent, and their cheap subway straps! *(Pausing for effect.)* That's what the real story of Anastasia is about.

(She crosses triumphantly back to her chair. For once, the company is speechless.)

BETTY/BAILIFF. *(Finally, breaking the silence.)* Where are we?

AMY. *(Rising and crossing up right to exit.)* I'm leaving!

BETTY/BAILIFF. *(Intercepting her.)* No, you're not!

AMY. Oh, come on, Betty.... You're not even an actor. You're just a stupid, fucking stagehand.

BETTY/BAILIFF. No! I *am* an actor! *(Appealing to the audience.)* I'm the Bailiff! I'm the Bailiff…. *(She looks at AMY, looks back at the audience, and then closes her eyes and takes a deep breath. AMY, confused, watches her. Slowly, BETTY opens her eyes.)* I *am* the Bailiff. *(She smiles as if waking up from a dream and looks around the stage.)* I'm the Bailiff. And this … *this* … is my courtroom. This is *my* courtroom. *(She turns calmly and addresses AMY pleasantly, but with absolute authority.)* And you *will* sit your ass down, Baroness. *(AMY, nonplused, turns abruptly and sits.)* And now … *(Turning toward the defendants, who duck.)* the Bailiff would like to hear from … *(ATHENA catches her eye and points at LISA.)* Zinaida Tolstoy!

LISA. *(Her play already in a shambles, LISA throws up her hands.)* Why not?

(She crosses to the witness chair.)

BETTY/BAILIFF. *(Crossing up to her.)* Do you swear—
ATHENA/DEFENSE ATTORNEY. *(Rising and taking charge.)* She's still under oath.
BETTY/BAILIFF. Oh ….

(She crosses back to her stool. Her moment is over.)

ATHENA/DEFENSE ATTORNEY. *(To LISA.)* You told us earlier that you nursed the plaintiff at a time when she was under sedation.
LISA/ZINAIDA TOLSTOY. Yes.
ATHENA/DEFENSE ATTORNEY. And that during that time she told her story.
LISA/ZINAIDA TOLSTOY. Yes.
ATHENA/DEFENSE ATTORNEY. And did she tell you about

her marriage to the soldier who rescued her?

LISA/ZINAIDA TOLSTOY. Yes.

THENA/DEFENSE ATTORNEY. And did she tell you her reason for marrying him?

LISA/ZINAIDA TOLSTOY. She was five months pregnant at the time of the massacre. She wanted the baby to have a legal father.

ATHENA/DEFENSE ATTORNEY. And did she tell you where her son is?

DIANE/PROSECUTING ATTORNEY. *(Rising.)* Objection!

ATHENA/DEFENSE ATTORNEY. On what grounds?

DIANE/PROSECUTING ATTORNEY. On the grounds that this was not in the original script, and I have not had time to prepare a defense.

THENA/DEFENSE ATTORNEY. May I remind you that your client is the plaintiff. I am the one doing the defending.

DIANE/PROSECUTING ATTORNEY. *(To LISA.)* I want this struck from the record. I can't believe you would allow the defense to manipulate an audience this way—judging a rape victim for abandoning the child born of that rape.

ATHENA/DEFENSE ATTORNEY. May I remind you that during Clara Peuthert's testimony, the prosecution contended that my client's personal history was no excuse for her behaviors toward a person under her care.

DIANE/PROSECUTING ATTORNEY. How could my client, a child herself—wounded, mentally ill, hiding for her life, possibly be expected to care for—or even care about—the by-product of her rape?

ATHENA/DEFENSE ATTORNEY. By-product? So here we have a dehumanization of the baby simply because of the political circumstances surrounding his conception. Much in the same way, I might add, that the Bolsheviks dehumanized the children of the Tsar in light of the wholesale and historic rape of the common people that had been going on for centuries under the tyrannical rule of the tsars. But that's different, isn't it? Could there be some gender bias in your argument, counselor?

MARIE. Oh, look who's talking!

DIANE/PROSECUTING ATTORNEY. It has been my observation that the gender of soldiers and rapists is remarkably consistent.

ATHENA/DEFENSE ATTORNEY. Is the Women's Court going to adopt a different code of ethics regarding the treatment of male children?

DIANE/PROSECUTING ATTORNEY. Athena, you know very well that is not the issue here.

ATHENA/DEFENSE ATTORNEY. Well, then perhaps you will allow me to finish my examination of Baroness Tolstoy, so that you can tell us what that issue is.

(DIANE sits.)

ATHENA/DEFENSE ATTORNEY. Zinaida, can you tell us where Anastasia's son—excuse me—where her *child* is?

LISA/ZINAIDA TOLSTOY. No one knows.

ATHENA/DEFENSE ATTORNEY. Not even the mother?

LISA/ZINAIDA TOLSTOY. No. She left him in Rumania.

ATHENA/DEFENSE ATTORNEY. Did the community of Russian emigrants know about the baby?

LISA/ZINAIDA TOLSTOY. They had heard the rumors of the marriage and the child.

ATHENA/DEFENSE ATTORNEY. And how did they respond?

LISA/ZINAIDA TOLSTOY. They were very concerned about who was next in line for the throne.

ATHENA/DEFENSE ATTORNEY. Can you be more specific?

LISA/ZINAIDA TOLSTOY. If Anastasia was who she said she was—the tsar's daughter—and if the rumors about the baby were true, then every orphan boy in Rumania would have the right to lay claim to the throne of Russia. So you see, it was an impossible situation.

ATHENA/DEFENSE ATTORNEY. Was this the motive behind the emigrants paying a man like Pierre Gilliard to publish his book and give his lectures on the "false Anastasia?"

LISA/ZINAIDA TOLSTOY. Oh, yes. The movement was highly organized.

ATHENA/DEFENSE ATTORNEY. So this would explain why a woman like Shura might stop visiting suddenly—because her loyalty to Russia was greater than her loyalty to one Grand Duchess?

LISA/ZINAIDA TOLSTOY. Yes.

ATHENA/DEFENSE ATTORNEY. Thank you. Your witness.

(She sits.)

DIANE/PROSECUTING ATTORNEY. *(Rising.)* And you? What position did you take?

LISA/ZINAIDA TOLSTOY. I supported the family.

DIANE/PROSECUTING ATTORNEY. In other words, you sacrificed this woman's right to her identity because of your loyalty to the family name?

LISA/ZINAIDA TOLSTOY. If Anastasia had been loyal to the family name, she would have concealed the existence of the baby.

DIANE/PROSECUTING ATTORNEY. My client was loyal to herself, to Anastasia. Why should she be ashamed of herself, because of what other people did to her? If telling the truth about her life is disloyal to her father's name—that's not her fault.

LISA/ZINAIDA TOLSTOY. Then why is she trying to claim an identity based on her father's name? It's his money, his title, his country—isn't it? Women don't have any of these things by ourselves.

(DIANE doesn't say anything. There is a long silence.)

BETTY/BAILIFF. Shall I call the last witness?

DIANE/PROSECUTING ATTORNEY. *(To BETTY.)* No.

BETTY/BAILIFF. What's the matter?

DIANE/PROSECUTING ATTORNEY. *(Staring at LISA.)* She's right. *(DIANE sits.)* The playwright is right. I am asserting my client's claim to an identity that was never hers. I don't know how to proceed.

DONNA. It doesn't matter what the actor thinks. Diane, just perform your part.

DIANE. But how can I do that, when I don't believe in it anymore?

DONNA. Ask Diane. That's what we all do.

BETTY/BAILIFF. Hey!

AMY. Oh, for Christ's sake! It's just a part!

MELISSA. We have to finish the play!

DONNA. No, we don't. The great Diane Anthony is having a moral crisis, so we should all stop what we're doing and await the outcome.

DIANE. *(Confused.)* I don't want you to have to wait.

DONNA. Oh, well, then we won't. Just tell us what you want us to do.

BETTY/BAILIFF. Get off her case!

JENNY. *(Suddenly throwing off the coat.)* I've got something to say! I think you're all hypocrites—including you, Diane. *(She rises, throwing the coat on the chair.)* This woman is sick! *(Indicating the coat.)* She's sick! Do you think she cares about this court business? Do you really think she gives a damn about any of this? Do you think she wants to be here? Do you think a survivor like Anastasia gives a goddamn about whether or not these women are found guilty?

MARIE. *(Rising.).* Yes, I do. I'm a survivor, and I'll tell you something—I sure as shit would love to see all my betrayers sitting here in a court of women!

JENNY. What's that going to do for your pain?

MARIE. It's going to make me feel there's a little justice in this life.

JENNY. Yeah, well, I came here tonight so sick I didn't think I could perform, and none of you gave a goddamn about that! You— *(To MARIE.)* with your politics *(MARIE sits.)* or you—*(To LISA.)* with your precious script, or you—*(To MELISSA.)* with your critics, or you—*(To DIANE.)* with your big ideas about changing the world! Nobody gave a damn about me, so long as I didn't mess up your show. *(To ATHENA.)* And then Athena here—my pal—she tricked me into giving up the lead, so she could have it. But I'm still sick, and I still lost a lead role and I probably won't draw it again, and making all of you go sit in those chairs over there isn't going to make me feel any better or give me back my chance to play the attorney. And if I tell you all that you're fucked and inhuman and selfish—you know what? I'm out of a theater company. And Diane is having a hard time figuring out whether or not Anastasia deserved her daddy's money, but you know what? Anastasia isn't going to get it anyway, so who gives a shit? If she'd figured out what the score was in 1922, she might have made a new life for herself, but it was people like you— people trying to work off their own guilt—who kept her trying to be a Grand Duchess for fifty years, when there wasn't even any imperial Russia anymore. Don't you get it? It's gone. It's over. The kingdom we had as little girls, that we thought was ours, is fucking gone. It's gone. It went when the babysitter put his hand up our nightgown, it went when uncle made us suck his candy, it went when daddy climbed on top of us. It's gone. It's fucking gone and it's never coming back, and all the fucking courtrooms and trials in the world aren't going to bring it back. Never. It's gone. It's fucking gone. It's gone. It's gone. It's gone! *(She begins to choke with rage. DIANE rises and starts to cross to her. JENNY wheels around.)* I don't want your help! I want to be somebody other than a fucking victim before this whole thing's over and it's too late. *(A long pause.)* I want to be the prosecutor. *(DIANE crosses upstage. JENNY turns to LISA.)* And I want *you* to be Anastasia! *(LISA rises from the witness chair. JENNY throws the coat at her.)* Here! Be sure to put that over your head....

It's in the script! *(LISA crosses to ANASTASIA's chair, and sits, draping the coat over her head. JENNY turns to ATHENA.)* And *you*...I want *you* to be Annie Jennings!

(ATHENA doesn't move. BETTY rises and crosses center stage.)

BETTY/BAILIFF. The court calls Annie Jennings to the stand. *(ATHENA still doesn't move. BETTY takes a step toward her. At this, ATHENA rises and crosses to the witness chair.)* State your name, please.

ATHENA/ANNIE JENNINGS. Annie Burr Jennings.

BETTY/BAILIFF. Do you swear to tell the truth, the whole truth, and nothing but the truth?

ATHENA/ANNIE JENNINGS. I do.

(BETTY returns to her stool.)

JENNY/PROSECUTING ATTORNEY. Could you tell us about your relationship to the plaintiff?

ATHENA/ANNIE JENNINGS. During the Grand Duchess' visit to New York, I entertained her in my home.

JENNY/PROSECUTING ATTORNEY. Aren't you being a little modest, Miss Jennings? Hadn't you invited the Grand Duchess to come and live with you on a permanent basis?

ATHENA/ANNIE JENNINGS. *(Hedging.)* The original offer of hospitality had been open-ended.

JENNY/PROSECUTING ATTORNEY. But it certainly became close-ended, didn't it?

DIANE/DEFENSE ATTORNEY. *(Rising.)* Objection.

JENNY/PROSECUTING ATTORNEY. Withdrawn. *(DIANE sits.)* Miss Jennings, did my client travel all the way to America to take advantage of your hospitality?

ATHENA/ANNIE JENNINGS. No. She had come here to live

with a relative in Oyster Bay. But, of course, she was impossible and they had to ask her to leave.

JENNY/PROSECUTING ATTORNEY. And that's when you made your "open-ended" offer?

ATHENA/ANNIE JENNINGS. Yes.

JENNY/PROSECUTING ATTORNEY. But you knew that she was a difficult houseguest?

ATHENA/ANNIE JENNINGS. Oh, yes. Everyone knew that. She's out of her mind.

JENNY/PROSECUTING ATTORNEY. Then, I'm having trouble understanding why you would invite her into your home.

ATHENA/ANNIE JENNINGS. *(Smiling.)* In retrospect, I have trouble understanding that myself.

JENNY/PROSECUTING ATTORNEY. Then perhaps we can help each other discover a motive. *(This makes the witness uneasy.)* You're a wealthy woman, aren't you, Athena?

ATHENA/ANNIE JENNINGS. *(Firm.)* That's "Annie Jennings," and wealth is a relative concept.

JENNY/PROSECUTING ATTORNEY. But your father was the original chairman of the board for Standard Oil, wasn't he?

ATHENA/ANNIE JENNINGS. Yes.

JENNY/PROSECUTING ATTORNEY. Would it be safe to say that you are not without anything that money can buy?

ATHENA/ANNIE JENNINGS. It would be safe to say that I provide myself with the things necessary for my comfort.

JENNY/PROSECUTING ATTORNEY. And yet there are some things that money can't buy, aren't there?

ATHENA/ANNIE JENNINGS. *(With irony.)* Love?

JENNY/PROSECUTING ATTORNEY. And titles.

DIANE/DEFENSE ATTORNEY. *(Rising.)* Objection.

JENNY/PROSECUTING ATTORNEY. Very well, then. *(DIANE sits.)* There were rumors in the society columns that you intended to adopt Anastasia. Is that true?

ATHENA/ANNIE JENNINGS. It's true it was in the columns. It is not true that I ever thought of adopting her.

JENNY/PROSECUTING ATTORNEY. Really? That surprises me. Adopting my client would have made you part of the royal family of Russia.

DIANE/DEFENSE ATTORNEY. *(Rising.)* Objection!

JENNY/PROSECUTING ATTORNEY. After eighteen months of making Anastasia the toast of New York society, did you or did you not incarcerate her in a mental asylum?

(DIANE sits.)

ATHENA/ANNIE JENNINGS. You are—

JENNY/PROSECUTING ATTORNEY. Yes or no? Did you have this woman incarcerated against her will?

ATHENA/ANNIE JENNINGS. *(A pause.)* Yes.

JENNY/PROSECUTING ATTORNEY. Thank you. *(To DIANE.)* Your witness.

(JENNY sits.)

DIANE/DEFENSE ATTORNEY. *(Rising.)* Can you describe some of the plaintiff's behaviors at the time when she lived with you?

ATHENA/ANNIE JENNINGS. She spent money extravagantly. She had credit in my name, and she abused it. She was impossible to please. She hated her room, she hated the servants, she hated the food. She began to slander me, to say that I was a drunk and a thief. She had an enormous persecution complex. When she rode in the car, she would pull all the curtains down. She refused to see doctors when she was sick. She believed I was trying to poison her—she would only eat crackers in a sealed box. She began attacking people with sticks. One time she ran up on the roof with no clothes on. She would throw heavy objects out the window to attract the police. She spent all her time in her room talking to her birds.

DIANE/DEFENSE ATTORNEY. What made you decide finally that she had to go?

ATHENA/ANNIE JENNINGS. She began to talk about killing herself, and she was very convincing.

DIANE/DEFENSE ATTORNEY. Thank you.

(DIANE sits.)

JENNY/PROSECUTING ATTORNEY. *(Rising.)* You referred to my client as having a persecution complex?

ATHENA/ANNIE JENNINGS. Oh, yes.

JENNY/PROSECUTING ATTORNEY. Do you mean that she thought people were out to get her?

ATHENA/ANNIE JENNINGS. Yes.

JENNY/PROSECUTING ATTORNEY. And were they?

ATHENA/ANNIE JENNINGS. No.

JENNY/PROSECUTING ATTORNEY. Really? Were the Bolsheviks who exiled her, imprisoned her, raped her, shot her with her family, bayoneted her, and smashed her jaw, out to get her?

ATHENA/ANNIE JENNINGS. Well, I hardly ....

JENNY/PROSECUTING ATTORNEY. Was someone out to get her when she had to stowaway in the back of a hay wagon, desperately ill from her head injury, just to get out of Russia alive?

ATHENA/ANNIE JENNINGS. Yes.

JENNY/PROSECUTING ATTORNEY. Was someone out to get her when the entire community of Russian emigrants refused to identify her and left her to rot in a Berlin mental asylum?

ATHENA/ANNIE JENNINGS. Yes.

JENNY/PROSECUTING ATTORNEY. I see. But you think that she had a persecution complex. *(ATHENA begins to protest, but JENNY cuts her off.)* She refused to see doctors when she was sick. Do you have any idea how they treat women at public mental institutions?

ATHENA/ANNIE JENNINGS. No.

JENNY/PROSECUTING ATTORNEY. No, of course you don't. So she distrusted doctors. And she feared poisoning. Are you aware that the imperial family had to make continual provisions against being poisoned—that this was part of being a tsar's daughter?

ATHENA/ANNIE JENNINGS. I hadn't thought ....

JENNY/PROSECUTING ATTORNEY. No, Miss Jennings, you hadn't thought. And so one day a nurse and two orderlies—two *men*—came to get her, without any warning, isn't that true?

ATHENA/ANNIE JENNINGS. I consulted with three doctors!

JENNY/PROSECUTING ATTORNEY. Doctors who had never examined her!

ATHENA/ANNIE JENNINGS. She wouldn't let them!

JENNY/PROSECUTING ATTORNEY. And isn't it true these men had to break down the door, and that when they did, they found her cowering in the bathroom and dragged her away? *(ATHENA says nothing.)* I have one more question. Do you have any idea why she preferred the company of birds over people? *(Silence.)* That will be all.

(ATHENA steps down. She joins the other defendants. There is a moment of silence, during which BETTY consults her script.)

BETTY/BAILIFF. Believe it or not, it's time for the closing arguments.

JENNY/PROSECUTING ATTORNEY. *(Rising.)* Women of the jury—there is little I can add to what you have already heard tonight. These five women all recognized the Grand Duchess Anastasia Nicolaievna Romanov, and they all betrayed her. It is your duty to find them guilty of denying Anastasia her identity—a denial for which my client has paid dearly, and for which she will pay every day for the rest of her life. It is only fair that the Court of Women should hold these five perpetrators accountable for their actions.

(She sits. DIANE rises.)

DIANE/DEFENSE ATTORNEY. "Five *perpetrators*." An emotionally charged word to use in a room full of women. All right. Perpetrators. I ask you to look at these "perpetrators" now—Thea Malinowsky, Shura Tegleva Gilliard, Sophie Buxhoeveden, Clara Peuthert, Annie Jennings. Look at these women in the harsh glare of this courtroom. See them in all their humanity, removed from their environments, their motivations laid bare for your examination. How many of us would like to be them right now? To sit up here and be scrutinized for our choices in how we have dealt with the women in our lives? How many of us would come off looking any better than these women? Here are women who are desperately poor *(Indicating MARIE)* threatened with the break-up of their families *(Indicating DONNA.)* with the loss of employment *(Indicating MELISSA.)* with the loss of their very lives *(Indicating AMY.)* Women who acted rashly, or thoughtlessly, or—as in the case of the last witness *(Indicating ANNIE.)* with a great deal of agonizing. Women presented with situations in which all the choices were bad. Who can judge these women without standing in their shoes? I can't. I wish I could. I wish I could know that I would make different choices from these women.... But I can't.

(She crosses upstage, standing next to ATHENA.)

JENNY/PROSECUTING ATTORNEY. *(Rising.)* The question is not, as my worthy opponent has phrased it, whether or not we ourselves are guilty of similar betrayals. The question is, "Are we willing to be accountable for the harm we do to other women?" Let us dare to indict ourselves. Let us dare to say these words: "No more betrayals!" "No more denial!" Let us dare to look at the obscene choices with which we are confronted every day—to sacrifice ourselves or our sisters, or our daughters, or our lovers, and let us dare to say, "No!" And with that "no," let us force other options into being. Let us dare to make a new world! Because in asking that you return a guilty verdict against these five women, I am asking for nothing less. I rest my case.

(JENNY sits. BETTY rises.)

BETTY/BAILIFF. *(Reading from her script.)* Will the defendants please rise. *(The five defendants rise.)* Okay. *(To audience.)* Does the jury find these women guilty of denying Anastasia Romanov her identity? Green for innocent, red for guilty. *(She takes the vote, and then refers to her script.)* The Women's Court finds the defendants guilty [or not guilty]. *(She turns to DIANE, holding up her script.)* Now what do I do? That's all it says.
LISA. *(Removing the coat from her head.)* Adjourn.
BETTY/BAILIFF. *(To LISA.)* No sentencing?
LISA. This is the Court of Women.
MELISSA. So it's over?
AMY. It's over. And you can all find yourself another actor.

(She exits. After a long silence, MELISSA speaks.)

MELISSA. They voted against me [or They liked me]!

(She sits.)

MARIE. It's all about charisma, isn't it? It has nothing to do with equality.

(She sits.)

JENNY. I think they were just looking for scapegoats [or I think they just didn't want to deal with it].

MELISSA. What are we going to do about tomorrow?
DONNA. What do you mean?

(She sits.)

MELISSA. We'll never find an actor who can memorize the whole show in twenty-four hours.
LISA. We'll bring in someone to play Anastasia and the rest of us can use the lottery.
JENNY. So now we're going to assign a permanent victim?
MARIE. Business as usual.
DIANE. *(Crossing up to the witness chair and sitting.)* We can close the show. We can close the theater company. Or we can compromise.
DONNA. Stand back!
DIANE. *(To DONNA.)* It's not about me. It's about whether or not we want social change badly enough to violate our principles.
MARIE. *(Bitterly.)* It's about whether or not social change happens if we're violating our principles.
BETTY. Should I take the vote?
JENNY. What *is* the vote?
DIANE. "Do we close the theater or cast a victim?"

(This is a sobering moment for the cast. There is a collective silence.)

BETTY. *(Stepping forward.)* All in favor of closing the theater say aye.
MARIE. *(Militant.)* Aye!
JENNY. Aye.
MARIE. Diane?
DIANE. I have to abstain. I don't know what's right anymore.
BAILIFF. All in favor of keeping it open.
DONNA. Aye!

MELISSA. Aye!

LISA. Aye.

MARIE. So it looks like we go mainstream.

ATHENA. Wait a minute. I haven't voted.

MARIE. I think we all know where the rich man's daughter stands.

ATHENA. Don't deny me the opportunity to change, Marie. Or is that the prerogative of the Women's Court?

DIANE. I recognize that right, Athena.

(The two adversaries take a long look at each other.)

ATHENA. I vote to close the theater.

MARIE. So it's a tie. Three in favor, three against, and one abstaining vote.

BAILIFF. Aren't you forgetting the Bailiff?

MARIE. You're right, Betty! We win! That's four votes to close it. *(To the audience.)* The Emma Goldman Theater Brigade is officially disbanded!

BAILIFF. No. No, it's not. I vote to keep it open.

MARIE. You what?

BAILIFF. I vote to keep it open.

MARIE. Traitor! The only reason you got to act was because we were using the lottery system, and now you're voting to do away with it!

JENNY. *(To BETTY.)* You're not going to empower yourself by oppressing someone else!

MARIE. That's right!

DIANE. *(Rising.)* No! No, that's not right! If we've got to be perfect, it's going to be a long wait between the acts. We have to start where we are, and we have to keep going, no matter what. It's no victory to close. Nobody learns anything from that. Nobody changes the world when they quit.

BAILIFF. That's right, and you know what? I got to act. I'm a techie, and *I got to act. (To the audience)* Show me some green, cause *I got to act!* Yeah!

(The actors rise to congratulate BETTY. Blackout.)

THE END

PROPERTY PLOT

ACT ONE

In the House:
A red and a green card have been handed out to each member of the audience, or left in their seats, prior to the start of the play.

Off right:
Script for Betty
Money for Betty
Set of rewrites for Lisa
Hat with slips of paper in it for the lottery
Coat for Anastasia
Battered shopping bags for Marie

ACT TWO

Off right:
Rewrites for Lisa
Script for Marie

THE COSTUMES

All of the actors, as members of the Emma Goldman Theater Brigade, wear black clothing that is supposed to be their own — that is, consistent with their taste, income bracket, and personality. The two attorneys should wear black suits with ties or scarves. For the play-within-a-play, the actors add the following costume pieces:

DONNA (as SHURA)
    1920's hat

AMY (as SOPHIE)
    Fur stole
    Diamond jewelry

MARIE (as CLARA)
    Tattered shawl

LISA (as ZINAIDA)
    Russian scarf

BETTY (as BAILIFF)
    Uniform shirt

MELISSA (as THEA)
    Nurse's hat

JENNY (as ANASTASIA)
    Long black coat

SET DESIGN

witness chair

platform

chairs

chairs

stool